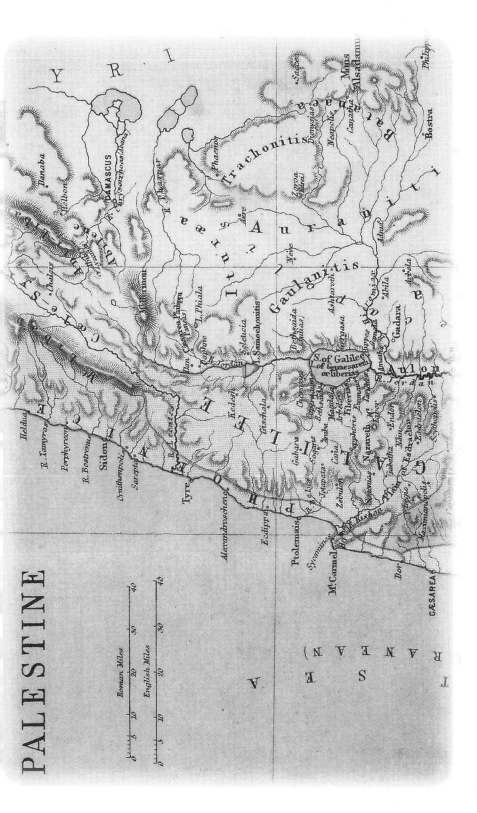

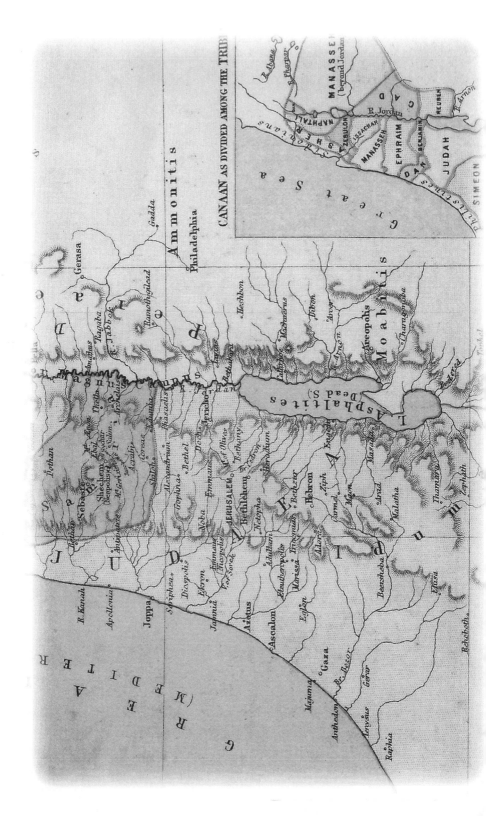

FOOTSTEPS OF ST. PETER

THE GOSPEL YEARS

JUDEAN CHRONICLES
BOOK II

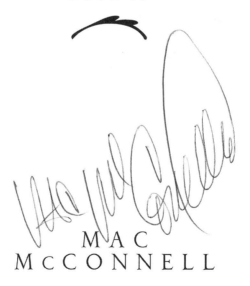

MAC McCONNELL

ONE WAY BOOKS

FOOTSTEPS OF ST. PETER

Unless otherwise noted, all Scriptures are taken from the Holy Bible, New International Version, Copyright © 1973, 1978, 1984 by the International Bible Society. Used by permission of Zondervan Publishing House. The "NIV" and "New International Version" trademarks are registered in the United States Patent and Trademark Office by International Bible Society.

Editors: Jodee Kulp, www.BetterEndings.org

Linda McConnell, www.OneWayBooks.org

Rosanne Hill Fine Arts, cover design

ISBN 978-1-9364590-4-9 (13 digit)
Library of Congress Catalog Card Number 2011917098

www.OneWayBooks.org — (954) 680-9095

FOOTSTEPS OF
ST. PETER
THE GOSPEL YEARS

JUDEAN CHRONICLES
BOOK II

OTHER BOOKS BY MAC MCCONNELL

Book I, The Early Years fills in missing gaps of Simon's life before Yeshua. What was it like living in Bethsaida, learning to fish on the beautiful Sea of Galilee, dealing with the Roman presence and the Jewish culture? Why would Simon move to Capernaum? What would have possibly qualified this man to be a disciple candidate?

Footsteps of St. Peter, Book I
ISBN 9780980045154
$12.95

Book III, The Last Years is the eyewitness account you have been waiting for ~ the foundation of all things Christian explodes. And guess who is at the forefront. Simon has become Peter, but more importantly he's the spiritual leader plunged right in the middle of heresy persecution, jealousy and false prophecy. But, does more for spreading the good news than even he can imagine.

Footsteps of St. Peter, III
Release Date: Nov. 2012

Why wold a nice Jewish boy grow up to be a despised tax collector in 1st Century Jericho? Then what would compel him to go out on a limb to see the latest in a long line of would-be Messiahs? Forever Changed brings the Biblical account of the renown little man Zacchaeus, answering a question of a lifetime.

Forever Changed
ISBN 9780980045116
$12.95

Cradle to Cross Trilogy

Joseph,
The Father's Journey
5 x 7 HC - 128 pages
Retail $12.95
9780980045130

Bozra,
The Shepherd's Journey
5 x 7 HC - 128 pages
Retail $12.95
9780980045109

Hadad,
An Innkeeper's Journey
5 x 7 HC - 128 pages
Retail $12.95
9780980045123

Joseph, Bozra and Hadad packaged together for the inside story of three eyewitnesses to the dangerous, romantic and traumatic times of 1st century Judea and the life of Yeshua.
The Cradle to Cross Trilogy will be an important addition to your favorites from Bible Actor Mac McConnell.

Cradle to Cross Trilogy Collector's Edition
www.CradletoCrossTrilogy.org
Retail $29.95
9780980045161

Mac's books are available at your favorite Christian
& on-line bookstores.
Bookstores please contact Spring Arbour,
STL-Distribution & Anchor Distribution.

WHAT THEY SAY ABOUT THE
JUDEAN CHRONICLES, BOOK I.

Mac has woven a moving narrative of Peter's early years, which leaves the reader aching for Book II of Footsteps of St. Peter.
Laura Groves

Simon Peter is perfectly captured in Mac's book with such innovation and with great, believable description, just as he has done on stage for years.
Dan Wielhouwer, Cornerstone University.

Mac McConnell has an incredible gift of bringing Bible characters alive through his writing and performances with a fresh taste of the scriptures. I can promise you that you will be rewarded for the investment you make in the Judean Chronicles!
Dave Condiff, Strang Communications

I'm amazed at the way your characters become so down to earth and real. Once again you have taken one of our precious Biblical friends and made us understand what makes him so unique.
Sandi Casteel

Mac has penned a marvelous and poignant story of Simon, a young man whose desire is to be all that he can be. He has taken the scriptures and brought them alive with all the sensitivity and beauty that life can hold. One cannot miss the parallels of our own lives in the life of this young man.
Susan Gaines

Mac does it again! The Footsteps of St. Peter presents a pre-Apostle Peter that keeps drawing you in. Mac's insight into the everyday life of Peter is both humorous and serious, but always heartwarming. Another Mac-classic.
Lou Lentini

WHAT THEY SAY ABOUT
MAC'S OTHER BOOKS

We read your books and enjoyed them to the max! You have been given a gift for drawing the reader to another place and time. We think you were even more electrifying this year in the Ft. Lauderdale Christmas pageant. It seemed brand new. Bravo!
Richard & Nancy Barnard

Mac McConnell is an experienced actor and master story teller. You will laugh and cry as you identify with the characters in these powerful journeys.
Gigi Graham

I have watched Mac perform for years and been mesmerized by his contagious passion. As I read his books I found myself laughing out loud, then warmed to my core at his uncanny ability to draw me into each character.
Dr. Bob Barnes, Sheridan House

I sat on that beach alone and as I read it, I wept. I needed to be reminded that Yeshua does heal the sick, opens the eyes of the blind, raises the dead, and above all heals the brokenhearted.
Lori Ferrara

Just as Mac brings characters to life on the stage, he transforms the written word into another world ... you won't want an intermission!
Janet Porter, F2A.org

Mac's dramas are captivating and his novels keep me turning pages until I was sorry it ended. Definitely a home run.
Brian Doyle, MVP 1978 World Series

DEDICATION

This is the perfect book to dedicate to my personal change agent. He accuses me of being too much like the Simon Peter of this book and then encourages me to be just that. My pastor for 17 years, Dr. Larry Thompson, would not take the credit, but he's the one who gave me the push, the drive and the challenge to get out of the boat.

Thanks, LT, I needed that.

FOREWORD

I've been asked numerous times to give an account—my story of three years with Jesus. But reasoned the Gospel writers didn't need my feeble input. It was Joanna, my precious wife, who encouraged me to at least offer a journal or memoir of my own. "You're his favorite, Peter," she reminded me. It took her years to call me Peter, she prefers Si. But Peter he named me and Peter is who I've become.

There's danger in these pages. Not the kind you'd expect. The kind that comes with knowing. When you know what to do and don't do it there are consequences. Is it better to avoid learning? I'll just say, I'm glad I didn't. You may think it silly for me to warn you against reading my notes, for you could change your mind and put it aside. I'll take that risk and implore you to proceed.

Jesus, was, is beyond explanation, yet made himself accessible to every level of humanity. He held his emotions tight, not deviously, and you would know his fury when confronted with evil. He could play with you, had an uproarious laugh, but would stare a hole through your soul when disappointed with pitiful faith. To know his full nature is not possible, but there is much you can and should know. He exposed himself, like looking through still water and seeing the bottom on a calm day. But it was a mistake to second guess or predict him, he did not live by mere earthly rules.

The hardest lesson for me was to realize that when he chose me, he chose to remake me. To turn me inside out. Perhaps, he had me turn myself inside out, which made it all the more painful. Yet, I wanted to do whatever it took to see a smile of approval on his rugged face.

This is how Jesus worked me. He asked once why I hadn't been to temple since my bar mitzvah. I told him because it was full of hypocrites. He said, "You fished the Galilee with other fishermen. Any of them hypocrites? Did you stop, or did you fish." What could I say?

I pen these words with one hope, that you might know this man better than before. To feel his presence, his pleasure and his power.

However, it's not my opinion that counts. Father taught me to form my own opinions before I accept opinions of others. That made all the difference.

Peter

SCENE ONE

From

FOOTSTEPS OF ST. PETER

THE EARLY YEARS

JUDEAN CHRONICLES, BOOK I

You never heard me say I hated God. I just have no use for him. He took my father when I was barely thirteen. He took my childhood and made me the man of the house. He brought a drought that wrecked my fishing business. He humiliated me, made me work for the Romans so we wouldn't lose the house.

The final blow came when my son, my heir, my hope, my joy, my reason for living was born dead. I was done with anything God. But not Andrew. He's such an embarrassment. Good thing we're brothers and I love him, or I'd fire him.

I tried everything to get Andrew to keep his mind on our business instead of chasing the latest would-be messiah. I'd hoped he'd found someone and fallen in love—he's so good looking—the eligible ladies always dropping by. But no. He preferred the company of Phillip, his inseparable friend from Bethsaida, so they could debate the meaning of life. I'll tell you the meaning of life. Work—eat—sleep—work—die. It's not complicated.

First it was the Baptizer. A whole new movement. The blabber was everywhere. The Essenes that Andrew and Phillip were so enchanted with—desert fanatics—found themselves a new front-man, a convert. Who knows what to believe?

"He's drawing crowds from all of Judea, Simon." Andrew never missed a chance to taunt me. "Phillip and I are going to hear him." He'd be all a-lather.

"Has he parted the Red Sea? Run off the Romans? Does he have a magic staff? See this?" I flapped a fish in his face. "This is what I believe. Nothing mystical here. This I can trust. Good God, the next thing you know, Elijah has come."

They were gone for four days—leaving the work for—guess who. And, talk about a shock, when they returned, not a word about this new rabbi, or whatever he is, this John the Baptist. Andrew went right to work like he actually meant it, as if he'd always done this. Maddening. I didn't say a thing. Didn't want to get him started. And another thing, Andrew didn't have to be asked to clean the nets, cull the fish or anything.

"What else, Brother? Just tell me. I'd be happy to." I felt his head to see if he had a fever.

"All right, all right, Andy, what is it? Have you been into the Passover wine?"

"What is what?"

"What is what? Who do you think you're kidding? All this work and no complaints. You don't have to be asked, you're not dashing off to study Torah, avoiding me, any of that. Have you lost your precious faith?"

"I have more faith in my faith than ever, Simon. It's more real than real. It's more, how can I put it, it's more honest than ever. It's more inspiring, joyful, and hopeful. I can feel it."

"Well, whatever it is, I can see it, Andrew."

"That," Andrew jerked his head, "may be the nicest thing you've ever said."

"What. What'd I say?"

"Simon, it's the Baptizer. We caught up to him across the Jordan at Beth-bara. There were hundreds there."

I was prepared for a spew of nonsense, but never saw Andrew so sure of himself.

"There were Pharisees—"

"Hypocrites."

"Simon, if you don't want to hear this, say so or keep that mouth shut and your opinions to yourself till I'm finished."

He knew better than to talk to me like this, but I let it go—no one heard him.

"Like I said, there were Pharisees—" I left it alone. "There were Romans. There were peasants and farmers, women, children and rabbis with their students. There were shopkeepers, soldiers and—prostitutes." I wanted to offer my opinion here, but Andy didn't take a breath. "There were beggars and temple guards, merchants and tax collectors. And the wealthy too."

"Andrew, I appreciate all the details, but could we agree there were all kinds there?"

"Yes. Sorry. It's just, I can still see them strewn across the shore standing, sitting, kneeling. John the Baptizer in the water up to his knees—"

"Andrew."

"All right, Simon." Andy's face reddened.

"Thank You." I leaned against our boat, put down the net and folded my arms across my chest—I felt like Father—ready to set the story straight. Something told me this might take some time. I was amused. Andy was excited, and for once—no lie—I wanted to listen. He moved up the bank and sat on a stump.

"Simon, let me say this, the man is captivating. To be honest he looked possessed, thin as an oar and obviously a Nazarite with uncut hair and full beard. They say he's been in the desert with the Essenes for years. It's hard to believe what you hear. Everyone has an opinion, like you."

I gave Andrew a deserved sneer.

"When he spoke, he had something to say. To everyone, every group. He spoke to me."

I rolled my eyes, but Andrew missed it—thank God—it's just a saying.

"Here's a man," Andrew said, "who doesn't care what anyone thinks. He speaks his mind."

"Like me?"

"More than that. He speaks his heart, and no one talked or left or nodded off. Even temple guards were enthralled." Andrew had my attention. "Simon, I can't do it justice. Some say, claim this man must be a prophet or the Messiah."

"Andrew. Don't jump to conclusions like you like to do."

"I agree, Si."

"You do?" This was a first. "Andy, what does this have to do with the new you?"

"Maybe this will explain it. He said, and Brother when he spoke, you listened. His voice boomed across the water like we were in a Roman amphitheater."

"Andrew." This could take all day.

"Sorry. If only you were there. He said," Andy stood as if this was his speech and bellowed in his deepest voice, "'you priests, you Pharisees, you brood of vipers, you hypocrites, you—'"

"He did not."

"He did."

"He called them vipers, hypocrites? Is he still alive? Did they arrest him? What happened?"

"I don't think they knew what to do. But if they tried to shut him up or take him away they'd had a riot on their hands. These people were ready to worship the Baptizer. Follow him anywhere."

"Tell me more." I asked for more? Unbelievable.

"Si," Andy sat, "the people asked, 'what should we do?' He told them, listen, this is great, 'if a man has two tunics, share with the one who has none. The one who has something to eat, share with those who don't.'"

"That doesn't sound revolutionary."

"Have you done that, Simon?"

"You're meddling. Go on."

"A tax collector asked, 'Teacher, what should I do?'"

"I'll be glad to tell you what any tax collector can do, they can—"

"I have a pretty good idea what you would tell them, but John told them, take only what is right and fair."

"I'll wager people were stunned." I was.

"Some applauded. Amens rippled through the crowd when a soldier stepped up, 'What about us, what should we do?'"

"A Roman soldier asked what to do? They give orders."

"That's what I'm trying to explain. Everyone was different, polite, even to each other. They hung on his every word."

"What did he tell the soldier?"

"No extortion. Be content with your pay."

"What happened to the vipers, the priests? Were they still there? Who could argue with this man?"

"My thoughts exactly. What he said we knew to be true. And for the first time the Sadducees and the Pharisees agreed when the Levites asked, 'Who do you think you are?' Simon it sounded like a trap, but John didn't flinch. Not for a second."

"Get on with it, what'd he say?"

"'I am not the Messiah.'"

"Well, that settles that."

"It gets better. They asked, 'Are you Elijah or the Prophet?'"

"What'd he say?"

"He said—are you ready?" Andrew leaned in, "He said, 'I am a voice of one crying out in the wilderness. Repent. The kingdom of God is near. Prepare the way of the Lord.'"

"Andy that—that sounds familiar."

"It should. From the prophet Isaiah—you're bar mitzvah verse—of course from a hundred years ago."

"Very funny. And you, who do you say he is?"

"I just want more of him. But I'll make sure I do my work and make you proud."

"Just who are you?" I had to ask. "And what have you done with my brother?"

Andrew smiled—a bit.

"I'll make you a believer yet, Simon bar Jonah."

"Don't get carried away with that, Andrew bar Jonah."

I wanted to spit—Andrew would not tell me another thing till I asked. He had me so curious that I did. I didn't regret it, well some. I worried he'd make a complete fool of himself, but he said, "I don't care."

But folks around town had gotten skittish about Andrew and Phillip and their rant about the Baptizer. And James's brother John was sucked in. Yet, they kept it under control. Andrew didn't act holier than me, but he was. He prodded and pleaded for me to come and listen too. If, and that's a big if, I did, it would be to shut him up.

"Why should I go, Andrew? You memorize everything this wild man says and regurgitate it back in a heart beat."

But it wasn't the Baptizer that had me worried. Andy said John the Baptist claimed there's another coming that he's not worthy to untie his sandals. We don't need another, tied sandals or not.

"He's in Galilee, no excuses, Simon. You owe me."

"Who's in Galilee?"

"The one John told us about."

"All right, all right. Soon."

"Promise me."

"Andrew."

"Promise."

"Oh, whatever."

"That's good enough for me."

I admit, what Andy said, I don't know, it was sincere. It counted for something. But he's my brother. I do owe him. I'll have to come up with a good excuse to avoid this—promise or no promise.

After a week I guessed Andrew gave up. I'd pulled our boat on the beach to plug that nagging leak in her bow.

"Simon, this is it. This is the day. Come." He hadn't given up.

"Andrew not now, not today." But I was trapped. "You see I'm right in the middle of—"

"Whatever it is, can wait. I will not take no for an answer. We have found the Messiah, the one the Baptizer told us about. You promised, Simon."

"I—"

"You promised."

SCENE TWO

FOOTSTEPS OF ST. PETER

THE GOSPEL YEARS

BOOK II

WHO DO I SAY HE IS?

Why today of all days, would a working man trudge anywhere to listen to some teacher babble about tired-out scriptures? Nets need cleanin'. Boat needs fixin'. No doubt this one's as full of himself as the rest. Yes, there'd been talk about the new rabbi—Jesus. Such a common name for a messiah?

"This one's different, Simon." Andrew called over his shoulder and took off up the hill. "You'll see."

"They can't all be different." A waste of breath.

I knew if I didn't go I'd never hear the end of it. I didn't keep up. What's the hurry? I should've asked Andrew why a messiah would come to Capernaum. I'll ask this Jesus myself.

There were twenty or so grown men around a man who sat on a boulder. I don't know what I expected, but this wasn't it. He could use a good meal and a more regal robe if he expects to impress me. I'd come up behind,

27

slipped to one side, and squatted. We were thirty meters above the Galilee—where I should be right now.

"Simon," Jesus said with a slow grin at the corner of his mouth, "you are the son of Jonah, but I will call you, Peter."

How could he know Father? Dumb, of course, Andrew told him. Call me Peter? That's not a Jewish name. I didn't see Andrew, but I saw stares from the rest. I should've said—what should I've said? Jesus left and the rest followed. I thought I'd join them, but why? I follow no man. This is a messiah? We'll see about that. Peter? I'll stick with Simon, thank you very much.

"Si?" Joanna stopped sewing as I walked through the door.

"I know, I should be working."

"You sick? Hungry?"

"No."

"No? That's it? All you have to say?"

"Jo, do you believe? Do you think—is it possible—?"

"Simon, sit. What is wrong with you?"

"If only I knew." One statement from this scraggly stranger cost me my ability to think. Me, the guy who won't talk to God, renamed by a messiah?

"You're scaring me. I haven't seen you like this since the drought." She has no patience when I'm not in control of myself and everything else.

"Joanna, Andrew took me to listen to Jesus?"

"You went?"

"He made me. I'd promised."

"Simon I know you'll figure it out. Your dinner is in the basket. Go fish, clear your head."

"But, Jo, this one is different."

"Are you listening to yourself? This is not like you. What will people say?"

She was right. A night fishing and this will make sense, or blow away in the morning fog.

I should tell you that Joanna went to temple on most Sabbaths, observed the sacred days, but that's it. She was relieved I distanced myself from things religious. Although she respected Andrew for studying Torah, that's where it stopped. And she's right, I admit, men look up to me. What will they think if I suddenly take up with some rabbi? My reputation is making it on my own. Toughing it out. I'm a self made man, and don't need a holy-man telling me anything.

The middle of the afternoon was early for fishing, but I went. Alone, to think. The Galilee was calm but my mind a storm. What if this, what if that, people will talk. Do I care what they think?—I do. I don't need this. It will pass. It'd better.

I stayed out as long as I could stand myself. The catch more than expected, but I didn't care—that thought rattled me. The other fishermen were busy when my partner, James, Zebedee's oldest, came to help me cull the catch. A big man, and makes sure you see the scar on his arm to prove who survived that fight.

"Simon, you're quiet."

"James, what do you think of this Jesus?"

"Is that what it is? Is that what has you acting so—"

"What are you talking about? I just asked a question."

"Oh? You just asked a question? The question on everyone's mind. So, Simon what do you want to know?"

"You know what," I shoved James to the ground, "never mind." He knocked my legs out from under me.

"Sorry I brought it up." I said as men laughed. We did too and helped each other up. Both to old for this.

"Simon, all I know, your brother and mine are spellbound by this man. Ready to follow him to the ends of the earth. But, I must say, John hasn't done one thing that has me concerned—yet. Now, if any coins disappear, I'll put a stop to it."

"Your brother asked for money?"

"No. Truth is, he hasn't asked for anything. And have you noticed, John is showing up on time, doing all that's expected, and hasn't missed a day? Simon, he even offered to scrape the hull of both boats."

"You're telling me nothing. Andrew's the same. Makes me crazy. It's like he can't wait to do something he never would unless I told him to. He just does things. James, I came down to the shore the other day and the nets were folded, ready to go. Andy sat reading his precious Torah like this was the most normal thing in the world."

"What'd you do?"

"Went fishing."

"Andy?"

"Went fishing. Get this, he said, 'Simon, did I ever thank you for taking care of me. For being my big brother?'"

"Is that a problem?"

"I see your grin. What'd you do if John said that?"

"He did. I gagged. But, that's the thing, it must be Jesus. Or that Baptizer. Whatever it is I can't complain."

"I went to see him."

"Him who?"

"Jesus."

"Something you need to tell me?"

"James, cut me some slack or you're going down, again."

"Oh, I'm so scared. Well, let's, uh, over here. No need drawing more attention." We walked up the beach, dragged the nets and stretched them out.

"So?" James said.

"I don't know."

"You always know. At least you think you do."

"Thanks."

"What'd you expect? Look, you're a good man. As headstrong as they come, but honest. And you should know, respected, and the best friend I could want."

"Thanks, James I feel the same. It's, well, it's like Andy said, there's something different about this man."

"You're not—"

"I don't know what I am, but I need you to be my friend right now. Can you do that?"

"Of course, but as your friend, do I need to remind you, you're an influence on every man in town? They watch you, and expect you to be right."

"That's not fair."

"Too bad. That's the way it is. And, if Simon bar Jonah is going to listen to this teacher from Nazareth and get all spiritual, then you can expect more than raised eyebrows and stiff shoulders."

"From you too?"

"No—I don't know."

"At least you're honest."

Not only did I not know what to tell James, I didn't know if I should. I wanted to tell him that Jesus called me Peter, but that might set him off. I wanted to tell Andrew—what am I thinking—Andy was there and hasn't brought it up. Had I heard wrong? What about the others that heard him? Not sure who most of them were.

Why is it, when life begins to make sense, something rips it apart? Father would slap me silly for the thought of something religious. Silly is what I felt. Joanna didn't want to hear it. James didn't want to hear it. And it's all I can think. I mean, there are things to consider. As Jo put it, "what will people think?"

As soon as I know what I think, I'll worry what others think. What about Father? Dead twenty years—hard to believe. What did his life count for? Nobody in Capernaum knew him outside of Mother, Andy and Jo. He hated religion. But his hate got him nowhere. I threw out God like an old net when I knew Father drowned in that ferocious storm the day after my bar mitzvah. What does my life count for? I'd better sleep on it. As if I could sleep.

THREE

This would be funny if it wasn't so ridiculous. Andrew and I were mending our nets one morning. Long overdue. He was better at this than me any day, actually enjoyed it.

Jesus came with seven or eight others on his heels. Will he call me Peter today? Andrew must've expected him. They hugged like long lost brothers and off they went. Phillip was with them and Phillip's cousin, know-it-all Nathaniel and James' younger brother John, the lanky one. I recognized a couple of fishermen, but not sure about the rest and was left holding the net when James came.

"Where they going, Simon?"

"You asking me?"

"Andrew left without out telling you where he's going?"

"Uh—guess he did. James, who are those men? Don't they work?"

"They follow Jesus."

"He has disciples—already?"

"Simon." Jesus waved. "Why don't you and James come too?"

James shrugged.

"Come where?" I said.

"The wedding. We're headed to a wedding in Cana."

"Hah. James did your hear that? A wedding? A bunch of grown men going to a wedding? They have nothing better to do?"

"You? What are you going to do?"

"Fish. What else? Ain't no fish in Cana."

"You like to fish alone?"

"You? You're going in the middle of a hot summer day?"

"Jews know how to do weddings." James had a point.

Oh, why not. A cool glass of wine sounds good. Wonder whose wedding? I should tell Joanna, but then she'll know I've gone mad. I'll think of something. But Cana's in the middle of nowhere, twelve–thirteen miles and a lousy road at that. It'll take half the day to get there and we won't just say Mazel Tov and leave. It'll be too late to fish when we get back. The whole town will know where we've been. This is out of hand.

"Joanna." Ut-oh. "I'm-off-to-Cana-with-the-others." I'll have some explaining to do.

Andrew dropped back and slapped my shoulder. A day without fishing might not be such a bad idea.

"Peter—Peter."

"Simon, that's you. Jesus is calling." Andrew said.

"I'm supposed to answer to Peter?"

"That'd be my guess."

I'd hurried up front.

"Peter. I'm glad you came." Jesus didn't break stride. "Do you mind if I call you Peter?"

"Does it matter?" At least he asked.

"Some."

"I've gotten use to Simon."

"I like Peter. You'll see."

What was I to say to that?

"Why a wedding? Why Cana?"

"My mother Mary asked me. She went to help her cousin with the arrangements. Mother loves weddings. What woman doesn't?"

"Good point."

"You like weddings?"

"Well, one in particular."

"Of course. Fine wife you have."

"You know her?"

"You'd be surprise what I know." Jesus was about to laugh but didn't.

What shocked us all when we topped the hill, all of Cana was there and then some. Jammed streets. Crowded shops. Children ran every which-way. Music loud enough to wake the dead. Tables lined down the center square. Servants dressed in white dashed up and down fanning flies off the platters. Everyone was dressed so nice and I looked like yesterday's catch.

"That's Mother." Jesus pointed to the lady ushering a man with a jug to the head table. "As you can see, she takes charge."

We followed Jesus through the middle of the party. I think they'd been at this for days. No surprise, weddings go for a week if the wine holds out.

"Come, my son, dance with me." Mary hooked his arm and swung him off to the crowd, looking too young to be his mother.

I sat and watched. Everyone sang and danced, ate and drank. The last I'd danced was my wedding day, but I couldn't resist and joined the throng. If Joanna saw me now she'd have me locked up. It wasn't long before I'd worked up a sweat and looked for a glass. But no wine— anywhere. I didn't want to be rude, but I was thirsty and knew someone should be embarrassed.

"Son, they have run completely out of wine." Mary took Jesus' hand.

"And, what does that have to do with me?"

"Please."

"Dear, Mother, I know you know I can fix this, but it is not time for me to reveal myself."

"It's my cousin." Then she told two servants to mind her son.

Jesus pointed the servants toward two water vats and they filled their wine jugs. I knew these were temple vats, ceremonial washing vats of water. Water—plain water. I thought the problem was wine, but the servants stared at the jugs, then at each other. They rushed to the wine steward. He took a sip and served the bridegroom.

"Wonderful, this is wonderful," the bridegroom tried to stand. What would be wonderful about water? Could he be too drunk to tell the difference between wine and water?

I told you, I was hot and thirsty, so I had to try this—water—myself. The servants filled the pitchers, I grabbed a glass and poured it full. My mouth so dry I didn't care about wine anymore, just needed something. I sloshed back a gulp of the best wine my throat ever knew. I wiped my mouth, looked at the glass—amazed—filled it again and flung it back. I'd never heard of a host saving the best for the last. Wait, this came from the vats. Water vats. Plain water into fine wine—that's a miracle.

"Simon." Andrew yanked my sleeve.

"What?"

"We're leaving."

"So soon?"

Now, I'd been awestruck, but this was beyond that. Was I the only one that saw this? No, we all did. Jesus said if we knew what was good for us we'd keep this to ourselves. He didn't put it like that, but that's what he meant. Two glasses of wine and my head spun.

Water into wine had some serious commercial potential. It's good I was there.

Joanna? How will I tell her? If only she'd tasted the wine, this would be a done deal. But if I tell her she'll say—I can hear her now—*You've come up with the wildest excuse to get sloshed in the middle of the day. You have been drinking that's obvious. But now you're delirious. Water into wine? Simon, that's the best you can do?*

And I ain't supposed to tell anyone anyway. It matters what she thinks. I'm scared of what I'm thinking. I should talk to Andrew. But I don't want to talk to Andrew. He's no doubt got an *I told you so* on the tip of his tongue. Maybe James, he was there. What—about—God? It's been too long. Was he there? What would I say? Would he want to hear from me, remember me?

Joanna was asleep when I got home, but first thing the next day.

"Joanna, Jesus is speaking in temple today, come with me."

"I should go to see what's the fuss. But, Mother is not herself, fever I think, you go. Change first, you look a fright. I don't want people thinking—what am I think-ing—when they see you, they won't know what to think. Don't forget your prayer shawl."

The whole town was there. I got suspicious looks and glared right back. They weren't any more righteous than me—maybe some. My first time in any synagogue since my bar mitzvah.

Capernaum's synagogue, the largest in Galilee, was not large enough for this horde. I doubted all were here for Sabbath. There're here to see what our rabbi will do about Jesus.

Murmurs filled the place. Dust filled the place. Ten-sion thick as chum in a feeding frenzy. Pretentious busy-bodies packed the lower floor, flaunting their fancy tallits.

I made it to the balcony and pushed to the rail. The Shofar sounded and Jesus went to the podium with no introduction. He looked at me with the slightest grin, then at the massive scroll placed on the podium by two scribes. Silence. Jesus rolled out the scroll, the students held each end. He held his palms over the parchment.

"A voice of one crying out in the wilderness." Jesus' voice filled the temple, "Be prepared for the coming of the Lord. Make straight paths in the wilderness a highway for our God."

Jesus pointed to another scroll, stepped back, and waited. The students rolled up the first and fetched the next. I spotted Andrew and knew what he was thinking, my bar mitzvah scripture I thought was nothing more than a ceremony haunted me again. Now if the next scroll is—

"See, I will send my messenger who will prepare a way before me. Then the Lord you seek will come to his temple. The messenger of the covenant, whom you desire, will come, says the Lord Almighty. Repent, the ..."

I couldn't breathe. My bar mitzvah verses in full. I grabbed the rail or would've collapsed. I waited. Not a murmur. I wondered if he meant it to sound so personal, as if he was talking about himself. I looked at as many faces as I could when the ruckus began.

"What do you want with us?" The madman screeched as he broke through the spectators. We hadn't seen him in months. I'd thought him dead.

"Have you come to destroy us?" He was filthy and scrawny, flailing his arms and cackling at Jesus. "I know who you are, Holy One of God."

Everyone backed against the walls. But not Jesus.

"Be quiet." Jesus said and the madman lunged at him.

"Come out." Jesus pointed one finger in his face and the man flopped on his back in a fit. Shaking. Twitching. Trembling. One last shriek and he laid flat. Dead?

Jesus offered his hand. He took it, raised to his knees then bowed at Jesus' feet. Jesus lifted him again as the chatter began. I watched amazed with the strangest sense of pride—then regret—wishing Joanna was here.

I went down the back to get her. It's not too late. Maybe Jesus would teach some more—who could know what he'll do?

"Joanna, can you come to—"

"Simon, Mother is so sick. I don't know what to do. Run, get the doctor. She's delirious."

"But—"

"Simon hurry."

Can you believe my luck? So close. I just wanted Jo to see what I saw. To hear the things he said. To feel what I felt. Her mother will be fine.

"Simon Peter, where are you going?" Jesus was with Andrew and James and John and others.

"To town. My mother-in-law Eda is sick. Joanna's in a panic, I need to—"

"Maybe I can help." Jesus started toward our house.

Perfect. This is perfect. But what if he can't do anything. Ridiculous, of course he can. Water into wine, a crazy man is in his right mind, no doubt he can cure a little fever. But, there is a lot riding on this. His reputation. My hopes. Joanna's mother. I think I'm the one who's loosing his mind.

"Simon?" Joanna shouted through the window. "Where's the doctor?"

I was in big trouble if this doesn't work. Jesus went in and everyone followed. I watched from outside. The house was full and Joanna looked like she would faint. Jesus went to Eda's bedside. I couldn't stand it, climbed through and pushed in. Eda was lifeless. Soaked. Pale as bee's wax. Was she breathing? Joanna dipped a cloth for her mother's head. Jesus touched Eda's hand and instantly her eyes blinked. Joanna gasped. Jesus lifted Eda's hand and she sat straight up, swung her legs around and stood. Joanna dropped on the bed and clasped her hands to her face as tears poured through her fingers.

"Oh my," Eda smoothed her hair, "all these folks here and I look a mess and there's nothing to eat." She headed to the kitchen. "I'll have something before you know it. Make yourself at home."

"Simon," Joanna hugged me, "did you see that?"

"Yes." I tried not to sound smug.

"That's a miracle."

"Yes." A little smug.

FIVE

"Simon, you're right, I understand." Was all Jo said as she darted off to help her mother, but it was enough.

I thanked God that he so quickly showed her what I'd seen. An amazing peace filled me. That was new and felt good, but I didn't understand it. I sat and watched these people flood into our house and out to our yard. Joanna and Eda served breads and figs and dried goat meat. The room filled with talk and dust and strangers and I didn't care one bit.

"Simon, who are all these people?"

"James, sit. I don't know half of them, but here they are."

"They sure are loving the food."

"No surprise. Eda and Jo are the best cooks in Capernaum. This gut didn't come from eating just fish. Look at all these people. What does it mean, James?"

"That you'll run out of food."

And we did. No, I didn't care about that either. But I did care that Jesus was getting swamped. They kept coming. Not just for food. Now came the sick, the cripple, blind, deaf and I don't know what all. Jesus moved to our courtyard and walked slowly through the crowd. He placed hands on each head, spoke softly, looking to heaven and then to the next. Some moved out back as more pushed through the front.

"You are the Son of God." A man screamed. The crowd scattered and pulled back. "You are the Son of God." Another man. "You are the Son of God." And another. There was nothing to do but watch and wonder. Mothers snatched their wide-eyed children and retreated behind the men. "You are the Son of God, You are the Son of God, You are the Son of God. Son of God—Son of God—Son of God." Over and over. Louder and louder. The three acted as one. They screeched. Taunted. But Jesus crossed his arms, stood his ground as the madmen swarmed. Then Jesus circled them in pursuit. The crazies laughed and jeered, as the crowd squeezed out the doors and windows. If I hadn't been entranced I'd of been frightened too.

"Enough." Jesus shoved his hand straight out. The madmen lunged, mouths open, but not a sound.

"Come—out—now." The men snatched their hands in front of their faces as if blocking the sun. They flopped to their knees.

"You are not welcome here." Jesus pointed to the door. The men shuddered, gagged and wretched but no vomit came. A cold wind swept through and the men stood. They looked at themselves—at each other—at Jesus. He looked exhausted as they left and the crowd began to applaud and Eda began to sing. I should tell you, Eda could cook, but sing—not so much.

Finally many left. Others bunched in corners or leaned against the house or trees. Jesus went to the roof as dusk crept in.

"Andrew, James, John, let's go." They looked astonished. "Fish. We need to fish, this bunch will be hungry."

"Si," Joanna tugged my coat talking barely above a whisper, "what are we to do with all these people? Where's Jesus? Where are you going?"

I don't remember ever loving Jo more than that moment. She was so tired and yet glowed like an angel in her nightgown, hair down, leaning against the door, yawning between her fingers with the gentlest smile and drowsy eyes. She takes my breath away. She'd worked all day without a complaint.

"Sweet dreams, sweet lady, we're going to show some fish who's boss."

SIX

No one wanted to fish, but I knew I wouldn't sleep. Moonlight glistened off Galilee while a family of rats scurried along the shore picking at fish bones. My faithful boat sat waiting for the punishment of nets drug over her gunnels.

"Fellows." I needed to light a fire under them, but not sure what was so urgent. "Glad you're here." I said instead.

Something was different—in me. The opposite of who I am or want to be. I knew I would live and die fishing—until now. I never felt like this and not sure I liked it. The closet thing to it was the day Joanna walked back into my life and I couldn't take my eyes off her. I just wanted to be with her every waking moment. I wanted to listen to her, talk to her, confide in her.

How can I feel this way about this man Jesus? Any man? Should I? Fishing is what I know. All I want to know.

My father was a fisherman, his before him. Being Jewish, meant family business. It's who I am. Isn't it? I despise men who don't know what to do with themselves. I certainly don't have patience for men who sit around spouting off spiritual blather. But, and please don't think ill of me, hear me out, this is new and I don't have all the answers, which I said is not like me. It's just that I could listen to this Jesus all day. I can't explain, don't ask me too, but the man is fascinating. There I said it.

Yes, the—the miracles are just that, but that's not it. When he does something unexplainable, remember the wine in Cana? When he did that, he didn't want anyone to know what he did. I think I told you he told us not to tell anyone. Doesn't that sound odd? That's what I'm trying to say, he's not normal. Anyone who could do that—if I could do that—everyone would know. I'd see to it. Then there was the lunatic in the temple. Remember? Well he's fine. More than fine, he's got a job. Returned to his family. Dresses like a sane person. Smells good—not that I care. Then there's my mother-in-law half dead and Jesus just touched her. Remember that? He just touched her and she jumped up and headed to the kitchen and made dinner for everyone. Are you listening?

I don't want you to think I'm crazy. I need you to understand it's not just me. He had this effect on lots of men. I told myself, not me, I don't need this. Fine for Andrew, he's drawn to holy men, to Torah school and the scholars.

But me? I don't know who I'm trying to convince. Every time I try to tell Jesus something, he looks at me with those smiling eyes. But now it's personal.

SEVEN

"Andrew!" I knew where he was. With Jesus. Can't say I blame him, but there's work to do. We need to eat. We have orders to fill. Bills to pay. It's not like I would traipse after this miracle man for the rest of my life. If he needs me I'm sure he'll tell me. But, I wanted something that made up my mind. Something undeniable. A voice from heaven would be nice. I mean, this is a man I could follow, I guess. What would that mean?

No voice from heaven, but close. I'd cleaned the nets. Not much of a catch. Who am I kidding? We had caught—close your eyes—tell me what you see. That's right, nothing, when here he comes—Jesus. Down the shoreline with the usual bunch. Do I really want to be part of this shabby crew?

Jesus came up to my boat at water's edge. His back to the lake. The group made a half circle and waited for Jesus to tell them something I guessed. I felt like the village idiot just standing beside him. Other fishermen threw down their nets and joined in. The next thing I saw, town folks trickled down too. Before long there was quite a crowd. Half couldn't see. How would they hear? The way they pressed in on him I wondered if they would dump him in the lake.

"Simon, I need to borrow your boat." Jesus said.

"My boat?"

"Yes, is that a problem?"

I fumbled with the nets. Tripped on an oar. Finally got the boat off the beach.

"Push off a bit so I can teach." Jesus climbed aboard as if he'd done this a thousand times.

The boat drifted out. I swung the oar over the side, shoved it in the muddy bottom and lashed it off. Jesus turned to the crowd, folks in front sat, the people in back could see and everyone could hear. I admit, it was perfect, but wondered what I looked like, what everybody was thinking, what I should be doing.

He told this story about a farmer. It's a little long so I'll give you the short version the best I remember. Why he picked a farmer while he sat in a boat around a bunch of fishermen is a mystery, or a mistake.

"A farmer went out in his field and scattered seed," he said. I wanted to say, isn't that what farmers do.

"Some of the seed," he said, "fell beside the path and birds ate it." No surprise here. That's what birds do.

"Some fell on rocky ground. The seed sprouted, but quickly withered and died in the heat of the day." I wondered if anyone cared.

"Some fell among the thorns, but the thorns choked them and they died. But some fell on good ground and produced a harvest a hundred fold."

Then he said, "Anyone who has ears, let him hear." I'm serious, that's what he said. I swallowed my laugh. This was not the most intelligent thing I ever heard.

"Simon, let's go fishing. Set out in the deep and let down your nets." Did he just tell me to fish?

"Simon, did you hear me?"

"Yes, of course." Should I tell him I have ears? I tried to explain. "Master, Andrew and me and the boys fished all night, and caught nothing." What I wanted to tell him, everyone knows this is no time to fish. I thought I should tell him, I'm the fisherman, he's the teacher perhaps he should mind his own business.

"If you say so." Is what I came up with.

What a waste of time and clean nets. Andrew climbed in and hoisted the sail. I turned the boat to catch the breeze as the nets slipped out. We made the circle, snatched the end, tied it off and began to pull them in. But when I pulled, the net pulled back. It was hung on the bottom—had to be. I pulled again and the water began to churn. Boiling. The net was full—of fish. I pulled again and the net began to tear.

"James, John, I'm up to my knees in fish." I hollered at the boys on the beach. "You better get your bu ... boats out here."

There was so many fish—jumping in the boat—flopping on the deck—till both boats took on water. We managed our way to the shore. It hit me, he does know more about my business than I do. We hadn't just caught fish, we might have caught them all. I felt stupid and ashamed. I fell at his feet.

"Leave me, Master, I'm a sinful man."

But instead he pulled me up. He put both his hands on my shoulders and looked me right in the eye.

"Don't be afraid, my friend. Follow me. I will make you a fisher of men."

I can't explain it. It made no sense. Maybe his voice, his size, the fish, everything, but I knew I had my answer. There are things in this world more important than fishing—must be. I laid down my nets ready to follow him anywhere. Yes—me.

"Come, follow me," he said to James and John. They waded to shore and left their old-man Zebedee in the boat.

"Simon, you stink." Andrew had a point.

"You don't smell like the first day of spring yourself."

We plunged in the lake, rinsed off and headed to the house to change. Joanna was waiting. What would she think? How will I explain that I'm leaving but don't know where I'm going or when I'll be back.

"Joanna, the Lord, he asked me to follow him." She held her finger to my lips. Was that a smile or a smirk?

"If it's the Lord, you better do it. Now come give me a hug."

EIGHT

"Simon, walk with me." There must've been twenty five men, and a few boys tagging along behind Jesus.

"What happened to Peter?"

"I said I *will* call you Peter. The day will come. Patience Simon."

"Patience is not my favorite thing."

"You're telling me? Simon you are about to witness great truths and see things few will see or know. You have the opportunity to learn secrets of the Kingdom of God. But it will take sacrifice, obedience and courage."

"Is that all?"

"For now."

"Where we going?"

"What part of follow me don't you understand?"

"You're not going to make this easy are you?"

Jesus smiled, but the words stung. He sounded like my father. What have I done? What will he expect? I thought he picked me because I'm Simon, a respected man in Capernaum.

"Don't doubt, Simon?" Did he know what I thought?
As we turned north toward Corazon, of all the dregs
in the world, we heard the familiar warning. The bell of a
leper. Then the chant, "Unclean, unclean." The voice was
hoarse. Then again, the warning, the chant, "Unclean."

I couldn't believe it. The leper stood in the street
wrapped in rags. Looking like a corpse. He's supposed
to yield to anyone till they passed when he's caught in
public. We have laws. He must be from the leper colony
east of Corazon. Then the smell. You cannot imagine unless you have been struck with the stench of a leper. The
smell of death and dying. Decayed skin falling off. Open
sores oozed puss. I'd rather pass a pig farm.

We stopped. Everyone knows, you touch a leper,
you're a leper. And lepers, if you don't know, are lepers
because of their sin. It's a curse. And it doesn't take a genius to figure it out if you touch a leper you're a leper and
people will say you're a sinner. Everyone backed away as
the leper dragged himself closer. Everyone except Jesus.

"Master." The leper pushed forward on his staff. He
stuck out his filthy hand. "If you are willing, make me
clean."

"Jesus, don't touch him, he's disgusting." I tried to
tell him. "Do you know what you're doing?" This had no
effect on Jesus.

"I am willing." Jesus took his arm. "Be clean."

The leper stood straight as a young boy. Jesus pulled back the man's hood. He helped him peel off the stinking rags.

"Bring me a robe." Jesus said and Andrew ran with his. We all came. The stink was gone. The man's arms—not a scar—not a blemish. His jaw dropped as he felt his face. His eyes filled with amazement.

"Now listen to me," Jesus said, "this is between you and me. Don't tell anyone what has happened. But do this, go show yourself to your priest and offer the sacrifices Moses commanded."

But Jesus did not tell me not to tell you.

"Men, I'm tired let's call it a day." Jesus walked through us and headed to town.

"Master, stay at my house tonight."

"Thank you, Simon." He put his arm on my shoulder. "I like that idea, it's been a good day."

NINE

I wish I could tell you how proud I felt. Jesus coming to my house. I wanted the men to know, but didn't want them to come, and they would.

What a day. He filled my net. They're still talking about that catch. Then he asked me, a fisherman, to follow him, the miracle man, or whatever he is. Andy said Messiah. I don't know about that.

I do know I haven't seen anything like this. And here I am walking down the street with this man that will stay at my house. I could be as famous as he. You know what I mean? If he's staying at my house, folks will know he thinks I'm somebody.

"Master, um, what should I call you?"

"You know my name. Some call me Teacher, some Master, some Jesus, and some say just a carpenter."

"But what do you want me to call you?"

"Simon, just call."

"Master, should we go past the synagogue then to my home?" They should see who's walking with Jesus.

"Simon, thanks for the advice, but you are concerned with the things of man. I'd rather we come in the back way, I've caused enough distraction for one day."

None left. We got home and they barged in, gathered in the court yard and outside of the low wall in the shade of the olive trees. Andrew grinned. I didn't. I wanted Jesus to myself.

"Simon? Again?"

"Jo, Jesus wants to stay here tonight, and we couldn't just tell them to get lost. They've been with us all day. What do we have to eat? I'm hungry and Jesus is too."

"What do you think this is—a boarding house? I don't have enough for all these."

"Did I say everyone? Just us. Me and you and Jesus. And maybe Andy and James and John."

"Joanna," it was her mother, "I can help."

"Joanna," it was Jesus, "do the best you can with what you have. You might be surprised, and I'm looking forward to your cooking."

I wasn't delighted with Jesus giving orders, but Jo and her mother went to the kitchen and the next thing I know they're back with plates and dishes and bowls of figs and dates and pomegranates and cured fish, sardines, loaves of bread and I don't know what all. Did she clean out the cellar?

"Simon, help pass these." Joanna had two plates stacked with flat bread and humus. "You know what to do."

"Where did this come from?"

"All I know is we have plenty, now please, take this and share. Everyone will think you're the best host, perhaps a hero."

Some night. Some left, but not enough for me. I saw Jesus slip outside and up to the roof. I bedded down on the bottom step so no one could follow him. Joanna was pleased.

TEN

"Simon, excuse me." Jesus climbed over me the next morning and went inside. The crumbled mess of humanity was amusing. Hot tea and cooking and fresh bread made my stomach ache.

"Si, wait on the others first." Jo handed me a plate of fish, but I helped myself on the way to the court yard. Jesus sat on the divider wall while more came and sat.

"Andrew, what's he saying?"

"He's been talking about Isaiah, the prophet. Shh."

"Shush yourself."

There were men and women and boys sprawled over every inch of benches and floor, leaning against walls and trees and each other. Children sprawled at Jesus' feet.

"The spirit of the Lord is on—" An entourage of puffed up Pharisees nudged through the men and boys. Some offered them a place to sit, but they stood blocking the way.

"Rabbis, take a seat, there are others here." Jesus barely looked up. They sat along the back wall and grumbled for all to hear.

"The spirit of the Lord is on—" Another ensemble of pompous priests assembled in the courtyard.

"Andrew, who are they? Where'd they come from?"

"How should I know? They must be from towns all around or from Jerusalem."

"If you will find a seat or move to the back so my followers can hear, I will continue." Jesus waited until they did. There was no room to stand anymore and I was thankful the courtyard was covered from the mid-morning sun. And that there was a breeze. The smell of men in the morning could ruin a man's appetite.

"The Spirit of the Sovereign Lord is on me." Jesus swept the crowd looking at each face. "Because He has anointed me to preach good news to the poor.

"He has sent me to bind up the brokenhearted, to proclaim freedom for the captives and release prisoners from darkness. To proclaim the year of the Lord's favor."

"We heard this in Nazareth." A Pharisee stood begging for an argument.

"Are you going to declare the same here as you did there?" Another said and they all stood

"If you heard it in Nazareth, what did you reason." Jesus did not stand which seemed to annoy the rabbis even more.

"Are you afraid to answer us?" A rabbi pointed a knobby finger.

"Do you see fear on my face?" Jesus said to every ones delight. Except for the Pharisees. They grunted and hissed.

"Who do you think you are talking to?" Another rabbi kicked up dust in outrage.

"You sir, this is my house," I blurted, "and you can take your cronies and—"

Splinters and thatching fell on the Pharisee's head. He looked up to get a face full. When more rubble fell we saw a gaping whole in my roof and four faces gaping back.

"What do you think you're doing?" I shook my fist.

"We could not get in for the crowd." They lowered a litter on four ropes. An arm dangled over the side as more thatching flitted down.

"Stop, you're going to crash on all of us."

"It'll be all right, Simon." Jesus said as the litter and a man with blank eyes, plopped to the floor at his feet. One of the four dropped down and crossed the man's arms on his chest. He took his legs and straightened them, but they curled right back. The cripple laid motionless except his chest heaved when he managed to speak.

"Sorry, teacher. Sorry."

There was obvious joy on Jesus' face as he saw each of the four men. First the one on the ground. Then the others as they peered through the opening in my roof.

Jesus knelt by the paralytic and put his hand on the man's chest, "My friend, your sins are forgiven."

The Pharisee's grumbling reached a new level.

"What do you think?" Jesus asked the Pharisee's front-man. "Which is easier? Should I say, your sins are forgiven or take up your mat and walk?" He waited. No answer. "So you may see for yourself and know my authority on earth to forgive." Jesus turned his back on the religious establishment, "Get up. Take your mat. You may go home."

The man looked at Jesus. His eyes now bright. He raised his arms and wiggled his fingers and laughed. He raised his legs. He bent them and straightened them again and again. He put his hands down and pushed up. He stood, then shuffled his feet, raised his hands, twirled and shouted, "Jehovah is God, Jehovah is God."

"Praise Jehovah." The crowd joined in.

The man picked up his mat and marched through the rabbis. They scraped their feet, huffed and left.

The lines were drawn. The new rabbi has spoken. Will he lead a revolution?

The crowd pressed in to Jesus. Children jumped with hands high for Jesus to pick them up. And so many questions and shouts of adoration.

Could I do anything like that?

ELEVEN

You would imagine, news about Jesus spread. We could not go anywhere without a crowd. When he walked through town people dropped what they were doing and followed. When I say people, I mean all kinds, and not just us Jews. There were shopkeepers, maids, cooks, young, old, children, tradesmen, innkeepers. I saw Romans and wondered if they were spies or curious. And women, all kinds.

"Andrew, isn't that—she's a harlot."

"How would you know?"

"Everyone knows. What's she doing following us?"

"Us? I'm sure she's following Jesus."

"Andrew, she's a sinner."

"And you?"

"You are comparing me with that?"

"Drop it, Brother. Just drop it."

We headed to the lake. Jesus said he had things to tell the crowd. I assumed he wanted to use my boat again. It was ready.

"Levi," Jesus said to the town's flabby tax collector, "follow me." I stopped, Jesus went on. Levi got up and followed. I couldn't move. A tax collector joins the group? He left his table, his ledger and tax money on the table with his dumbfounded assistant Perez.

I see a prostitute following Jesus. He calls a tax collector to follow him. What does that make me? I wasn't sure I should associate with them. A harlot is one thing—that's not what I mean—but at least she knows who she is and doesn't hide it, as if that would do any good. But, this Levi's been collecting taxes in Capernaum for three years and acts like he's doing us a favor. A Jew. I know that's obvious, but my point is, a Jew robbing another Jew and calling it taxes is just plain wrong. In case you don't know, and you should, tax collectors make their money by charging over the tax that's due Rome. That's how it works. We all know it. And Levi is rich—guess how that happened.

And get this, if you don't have your tax money on time he tacks on another ten percent. It's robbery. He's nothing but a thief. If you saw him, he joined in like he's normal or something. What have I gotten myself into?

I caught up to the others. Jesus waded out to my boat. He climbed over the stern and sat with his feet dangling in the water as the crowd sat or climbed in other boats. Apparently Jesus didn't need me. I'm not sure I needed this.

The row of men and boys on the shore of our curved harbor was over a hundred, and there were five times that many deep. The boats were full, maybe another hundred, when Jesus began.

"See these nets? The Kingdom of Heaven is like these." Now we're talking.

"When the net is let down into the lake it will catch all kinds of fish." Should I tell him we know that?

"Then you bring the fish onboard, you cull your catch." I wondered why he was having a fishing class. We don't need more fishermen.

"You divide your catch between good fish and the bad." This was not a surprise.

"Then you throw back the bad." We know, we know.

"So it will be at the end of the age. Angels will come and separate the good and the bad. The bad will be cast out into the fiery furnace where there is weeping and gnashing of teeth. Do you understand?"

Holy mackerel. He just threw a wet blanket on a perfectly good story. I'd gotten excited about a fish story and now he tossing folks in the fiery furnace. That's no way to build a following.

"Say, Simon."

"What is it, Levi?"

"Guess who's coming to dinner."

"What are you talking about? Why would I care who's coming to dinner?"

"You might when I tell you who. You might come too."

"Don't count on it, tax man."

"Jesus is coming to my house for dinner."

"Why would he do that? Why would he want to eat with you?"

"I asked and he said he wouldn't miss it. I don't think I'm working for Rome anymore."

"What will you do?"

"He said, follow me. I will follow him. Now, about dinner. You coming?"

"Si, dinner is ready. Your favorite."

She had everything ready. Candles, table in the courtyard. Her mother, no where to be seen.

"Jo, I'm going to dinner—with Jesus."

"Then you're going full. This is not going to waste. I have cooked all afternoon and waited to have a nice quiet dinner together. That's the least you could do."

"Jo, dinner is at Levi's"

"Dinner is here and now. Levi's?"

"I know, strange. Me having dinner with that man. But, that's where Jesus is going and that's where I'm going. I cannot miss this."

"Do you expect me to wait up?"

"All right, all right, let's have that dinner."
"Forget it. And I mean forget it."

I knew what I could forget.

TWELVE

Men came like ants to their hill. I elbowed my way passed some idiot who blocked the door and saw Jesus seated with Levi and it turned my stomach. Food platters were placed on every ledge and table. Servants darted around like bees. I waved them off at first, but the smells were too much to resist. I nibbled on slivers of dried beef and dates. My appetite raged. So, this is how the other half eats.

"Enjoying yourself, Simon?" It was—I'm serious—it was that cripple. The one healed in my house. He shouted over the clamor.

"It's you?"

"Glad you recognized me. How's the roof?"

"The one with the big hole in it? Sure are lots of people here."

"See that man sitting across from my Lord. That's the crazy man from the temple."

"No."

"And look at all the priests. They look like they're sucking lemons."

"Why are they here? Hoping to even the score? Is that, I'm sorry, what's your name?"

"Jannai. It means, 'he will answer.' And he did. I begged Jehovah to heal me, and he did. You were saying?'"

"I don't remember. Oh, is that—isn't that another tax collector? He's dressed like one."

"Another? There are a dozen here. Levi sent word he was throwing a party. He said he wanted his friends to meet Jesus."

"And there's that harlot."

"Simon." It was Jesus. "Sit." He pointed to the smallest place next to Levi." I shook my head. He nodded his. I sat down next to a tax collector who grinned for all he was worth—which was plenty. I should've stayed home. What was I thinking leaving Jo for this?

"Teacher." A Pharisee stepped up and the others close in.

"Why don't you sit and eat?" Jesus pointed to the end of the table.

"I, we don't sit, much less eat at the same table with the likes of these. I think you know that. And why are you eating with tax collectors and sinners?"

A hush fell.

I expected the stare from Jesus would burn a hole through the man. Others at the table joined him. James rose up on one knee ready to smack the man.

"I asked you a question." The Pharisee was impatient. That's a laugh, Pharisees were born impatient.

"It is not the healthy that need a doctor, but the sick." Jesus looked at the Pharisees, those at the table, and me. "Go and learn what this means, 'I desire mercy, not sacrifice.' I have not come for the righteous, but sinners."

"That's from Hosea, the prophet." Levi elbowed me, as I wondered if Jesus shunned them or shamed us.

"Teacher," some scruffy looking man in sheep's wool squeezed between the Pharisees, "How is it that we and the Pharisees fast, but your disciples do not?"

"Levi, who's that?"

"Must be John's disciple. You know the Baptizer."

"A long way from home."

"People just have to see Jesus for themselves."

"Levi, he called us disciples. Are we?"

"I am. Can't speak for you."

"How," Jesus began again, "can you expect the guest of the bridegroom to fast when he is with them?"

No one responded and I had no idea what he was talking about.

"The time will come when the bridegroom will be taken from them." Jesus swiped his bread in olive oil and shoved it in his mouth. "Then they will fast." He wiped his chin.

"Levi, are you getting this?" I said.

"I think he's—"

"No one tears a patch from a new garment and sews it on an old one." Jesus was off on another story. "The patch will tear. And no one pours new wine into old wineskins, or the new wines will be lost. He would pour new wine in new wineskins."

If anyone knew about wine, it was Jesus.

The Pharisees shrugged off and John's disciple left without a word. Jesus started a conversation with the prostitute behind him. She started to weep, but she looked happy about it—another mystery.

"Eat." Levi passed some plates. "Drink, there's plenty."

THIRTEEN

"Si, come to bed."

"You're up? I expected to sleep on the roof—again."

"You're choice, mister. Here," she patted the bed, "it's warm, and I am too."

Joanna's an amazing woman, and obviously forgiving. But it's more than that. What would I do without her? I told her what happened at Levi's.

"Joanna, Jesus called me, Peter."

"Did he tell you why?"

"Not really. And he doesn't call me that all the time."

"I don't understand."

"He said, I *will* be Peter. It was the first day that Andrew made me go listen to him. Then on the way to Cana. He said he liked the name, but the way he said it I knew it was more than that. Peter, it's Greek, it means rock."

"Well, you're Simon to me. Now come here, my husband."

"Jo, there were other tax collectors there. There were prostitutes there. There were priests there and a disciple of the Baptizer."

I wanted to tell her everything, but her lips shut me up.

Sleep was not on my mind. Fishing—my life—was not either. I'm not a kid yet felt this desire to spend all my waking moments following Jesus. But not with all those, how can I put this, those low lifes and pompous priests. Am I supposed to associate with harlots, tax collectors? And beggars, acting like they are somebody. It makes no sense.

If a messiah comes, it should be in the temple. Wouldn't he be royalty? Shouldn't there be angels? I neglected my recitations of Torah, the worse student, and for the first time I regret it. I knew there were scriptures of a holy one, but for the life of me can't remember much. It's just not logical that a messiah would hang around Galilee, dine with tax collectors, talk to prostitutes, or me for that matter. What does he want from me? I need to understand. If he wants me to follow him, then I need to know what to do. Wouldn't you? Why leave a thriving business and live day-to-day, not knowing where your next meal is coming from, to watch and listen to a teacher who doesn't care who's in the crowd?

He seems more at odds with Pharisees than with sinners. Where will this go? Real men take charge. It's what I'm good at. He should make me boss of something. Not one of the crowd.

FOURTEEN

The sun blasted through the window. I should have been up and out by now.

"Why'd you let me sleep, Jo?" I headed to the boat to see who was there—if Jesus was there. To get some answers.

"Brother," Andrew started south along the water's edge, "I waited. Let's go"

"Where?"

"Follow me."

"I've heard that before. Do you at least know where?"

"See the crowds?"

Remember my comment about ants going to the hill at Levi's house? Well this made that look like nothing.

"How did all these people know to come, Andrew?"

"You joking? They've been camping for days. You saw them."

We went to Tabgha, then up the hill making our way around groups and families. As we neared the top Jesus was surrounded. Men, women, children clung to him. That would make me want to head for the sea. But he touched and talked to them like his own. He'd been healing. There were staffs and litters and blankets and rags all in a heap. Jesus looked drained as the people reached for his touch.

"Ah, Simon, you're here. We can begin." Jesus motioned for the people to sit. "I have many followers, but today I call twelve for my apostles, to be with me and have authority to preach in my name, to rebuke demons and to set the captives free."

"Andrew—"

"Simon listen? This might be important."

"Simon. Simon Peter, I call you, my friend."

Was I awake? He called me? Apostle? Should I stand? Come forward? What?

"Zebedee's boys, James, John, I call you." They got up, should I?

"Andrew, you will join us of course. Phillip, you, and you Nathaniel." They embraced.

"The sons of Alphaeus, Levi, I name you Matthew. You and your brother James, I call you."

No. Tax collectors?

"Also, Thomas. And where are you, Cannanite? There you are, Simon the Zealot, join us. Thaddaeus and you, Judas Iscariot."

"Andrew—?"

"What?"

"An apostle? What's that?"

"I think it means we will follow, but one day lead. That's all I know. You need to think for yourself."

I knew Phillip, Andrew's playmate from Bethsaida. He moved here with his cousin and teacher Nathaniel years ago. I knew James and John of course and then he called Levi, but named him Matthew—here we go again. Levi's, that is Matthew's half-brother, shifty-eyed James, was new to Galilee and worked with Levi, I mean Matthew, collecting taxes. I have to tell you when Jesus called the Canaanite, another surprise. I remembered him lurking in the market when he bought my fish. But had no idea where he lived much less that he was a Zealot. But suspected that was a dagger poorly covered under his cloak. Jesus should change his name. It's not healthy to advertise you're part of the underground against Rome. Or, will we all be Zealots?

He called Judas last. He's as rich as Matthew from the look of his frilly shawl and did not associate with commoners. He dealt in imported carpet and such. I wondered if he—I wondered if we all will leave our work, our livelihood. Levi—or Matthew said he would.

I wondered about a lot of things. The crowd was ready to hear whatever he was ready to teach. This I remember.

"You who are poor of spirit," this was the first thing out of his mouth, "you are blessed." My mouth drop. "Yours is the Kingdom of Heaven." I needed to look like I knew what he meant—I was being watched—an apostle and all. "You who mourn you will be comforted." Jesus moved through the people. "The meek are blessed and will inherit the earth."

"Andrew?" But Andy moved down the hill and sat with Phillip and Phillip's son Elias, who was eating grapes.

Jesus asked the boy to stand. He plucked a grape and held it in front of Elias's mouth. Elias ate the grape.

"Blessed," Jesus raised another grape. Elias took this one as Jesus said, "Are you—" another grape, Elias sucked it in his mouth and grinned as many chuckled, "who hunger," another grape, a gulp as juice oozed from Elias's lips. "And thirst," a grape, a gulp, more juice as laughter rippled. Another grape, but this one Jesus had to push in the boy's mouth, "for righteousness." Jesus laughed too as he took four more grapes and shoved them into the boy's mouth with each word, "You—will—be—filled." The crowd sighed. Elias was delighted. It was hilarious and yet I'll never forget it.

"Blessed," Jesus was on the move, "are the merciful, the pure of heart and the peacemakers. Blessed are you when you are insulted or persecuted because of me. Rejoice, your reward in heaven is great."

I need to tell you the mountain side was covered with men, and families. But somehow they seemed to hear each word. Let me ask you, have you ever met someone you admire so much you wanted to hug him? I mean he was in command as he walked and talked like this was one big happy family, his family. Sorry, back to what he said next. Now don't quote me, I didn't write all this down—it's what I remember—best I can do.

"You are the salt of the earth," he said to no one in particular, "but if your salt loses its taste, throw it out, it's useless. You are the light of the world," he said to a couple of the disciples, I mean apostles, "let your light shine that many will see your good deeds and give God the glory.

"Don't think I have come to change the law or con-tradict the prophets." He faced the priests and Pharisees. "I have not. I tell you the truth, nothing will change until all things are complete."

The next thing, Jesus starts a list of you-have-heard-it-said-long-agos. But it sounded like he was doing just what he said he wouldn't—about changing the law. Judge for yourself.

"You have heard it said long ago, 'do not murder,' but I say, if you are angry with you brother, you receive the same judgment." That was hard to take.

"You have heard it said long ago, 'do not commit adultery,' but I say, if you look at a woman with lust, you have committed adultery with her in your heart." I heard groans. Mine the loudest. This apostle thing might not be what I thought.

"You have heard it said, 'do not break your oath,' but I tell you, don't make an oath at all. Let your yes be yes, and your no be no. Anything beyond that is evil." Jesus might have some wishful thinking with that one. I agreed, don't get me wrong, but there aren't but a few of us honest men left.

"You have heard it said," Jesus pulled Thomas to his feet, "'an eye for an eye, and a tooth for a tooth,' but I tell you if someone," Jesus slapped Thomas—it was playful but Thomas jerked his head like he'd been clobbered, which got a gasp or two, "slaps your right cheek, turn the other also." I choked on that one, wasn't alone, and tempted to tell Jesus if someone slaps me, I'll deck 'em. But decided to keep this to myself—for now.

Jesus added—you may not trust me—he said if someone sues you for your tunic, give him your cloak as well. I told you this was strange. Wait, it gets worse.

"If someone forces you to go a mile," he said, "go two. Don't turn away a man who needs to borrow." I should tell Jesus, he might want to hold off a little or he's about to run off the wealthy that he might need to lean on for offerings. But he piled it on.

"You have heard it said, 'love your neighbor and hate your enemy,' but I say, love your enemies." And I say that will drive your enemies crazy. He might be on to something. I laughed and got annoyed looks.

"Pray for those who persecute you," he was not letting up, "that you will be sons of your Father in heaven. Why? If you love those who love you, so what? The pagans do that" I agree he had a point, but—

"Be careful." I swear I could hear him just as good with his back to me. It made no difference. "Don't do your acts of kindness to be seen by men. If you do, you have received your reward already."

Could that be right?

"When you give, don't let your left hand know what your right hand is doing. Then your Father in heaven will reward you."

I admit that made sense, but who would've thought it?

"Master," Phillip interrupted. This can't be good. "How should we pray?" But Jesus looked pleased.

"When you pray, don't be like the hypocrites. They love to stand in the synagogues and in the streets to be seen by all."

The priests stared at their feet.

"I tell you the truth, they have received their reward in full."

Huh?

"When you pray, don't babble like pagans who think their god hears them because of their many words.

Instead, pray like this," Jesus looked straight up as if he saw who he prayed to. "Our Father in heaven, holy is your name."

I don't mean to interrupt, but did you notice, he said, "*Our* Father?"

"May your kingdom come, your will be done on earth as it is in heaven." As you guessed, silence, not a breath.

"Give us today our daily bread."

"Simon," Andrew punched me.

"Where'd you come from?"

"That's to remind us of when our ancestors were in the wilderness and God sent manna from heaven everyday."

"Andrew, I'm listening."

"Forgive us or debts," Jesus prayed, "as we forgive our debtors. Lead us not into temptation and deliver us from the evil one."

I can't speak for others, but this was the simplest prayer I'd ever heard. It may have been the first prayer I understood. Something else, I had no idea you could talk to God like he was listening. I guess I have a lot to learn about this apostle business. Some Pharisees left—during the prayer—must have been. I assumed we were done—but no.

"If you forgive men when they sin against you, your heavenly Father will forgive you. But if you do not forgive, your heavenly Father will not forgive you."

An amazing statement. The rules and regulations I knew were do's and don'ts, mostly don'ts, and then a sacrifice or two, and all is well. Here he asked me to do the reverse of what I'd do. But could I argue? It made sense to this fisherman. Some things he said I didn't care about and some things went against everything I thought was important.

He said when you fast don't let anyone know. I guessed he meant it's no one's business.

He said don't store up your treasures here on earth, but in heaven. He said, what will it profit you to gain the whole world and lose your soul? That would make anyone think. No, I had no idea how to do that.

He said, you might not believe this, but he said don't worry about your life, what to eat or drink, or even what your wear that your heavenly Father can take care of you.

He said don't worry about tomorrow, you have enough to worry about today. At least I can worry about today.

"Judge not," Jesus said. "The way you judge others, your heavenly Father will judge you."

This sunk in when he added, "Do unto others as you would want them to do to you. Do this, for it sums up the Law and the Prophets."

That could change everything. What, I wondered, would this world be like, if we held ourselves up to the standards that we expected from others?

"Ask," Jesus said, "it will be given unto you. Seek, you will find. Knock, doors will be opened for you." He stopped. This is just my opinion, but it looked like he'd lost hope that what he said was making a difference. Yet, he went on.

"Enter through the narrow gate. For wide is the way to destruction and many will go that way. Not every one who says to me Lord—Lord will enter the Kingdom of Heaven, but only those who do the will of my Father in heaven."

Two more Pharisees swirled their tallits and stomped off. Something got under their holy skin.

"Watch for false prophets." Jesus stared after them. "They come to you in sheep's clothing, but they are wolves." The priests should have heard that, and the approval from the crowd.

More importantly, Jesus called himself Lord. And he said, *my* Father in heaven. That ain't all, listen to this.

"Many will say, 'Lord—Lord, did we not prophesy in your name?' I will tell them, I never knew you. Away from me, you evil doers.'"

Jesus had taken this to a whole new level. He had a way of saying things, even when he told simple stories I was hooked. You didn't have any idea of where he was going. Nothing like the priests or scribes. Their dribble put you to sleep or made you sick to your stomach or hoping they would just shut up or pass out. They should take a lesson from Jesus. I didn't want to disappoint him, but he set such a high standard that I knew I'd do just that. One minute Jesus talked over my head and then a simple story—like this—

"If you hear my words and do what I say you will be like a man who built his house on rock. When the storm came and beat against the house it did not fall, because it was built on solid ground. But if you hear my words and don't do them, you are like the man who built his house on sand. The storm came and the house was destroyed."

See? Simple. Direct. I heard people agree, "Amazing—great teaching—profound—where did he get such wisdom?"

Jesus taught and talked for four hours and the only ones that left were priests and scribes. The ones who needed it the most, in my humble opinion. It looked like we might be here till sundown and my stomach was complaining when Jesus walked toward town.

"Pete, you suppose your wife has dinner ready—enough for me?" He didn't wait for an answer, but I'm sure he heard me gasp as dozens got up to follow. What will Joanna do? We'll need to hire some help and expand the kitchen at this rate. There must be a way to make some money from this. Gotta be. Should be able to make a killing. People have to eat, don't they? No crime in turning a profit. Of course if I could get Jesus to make wine from water we'd be set. I decided to run this by him.

"Jesus, I was wondering, got a minute?"

"Simon, I know I owe you an explanation about the net story from the other day. Is that it? I hope so. I get tired of folks telling me they have a better idea how I should use my powers. You have any idea how selfish people can be? Was that what you wanted?"

"Yes, the net story, that's it. How'd you know?"

"It just came to me." Jesus stopped.

Men behind stumbled into us.

"Watch where you're going." I told them.

Then I saw the centurion with two foot soldiers. What could this mean? The centurion dismounted, handed the reins to one of the soldiers.

"Lord," he knelt and quickly stood. "My trusted servant lies paralyzed and suffers greatly."

What, a centurion bowed to Jesus, called him Lord and asked him to heal his servant? Unbelievable. He bowed to a man who is not the king, not his superior and no one is holding a knife to his throat, defies explanation. And did you hear? He wanted Jesus to heal—a servant. Since when does a soldier give a hoot about a servant?

The world must be coming to an end. Can you imagine, a centurion bowing to a rabbi?

"I will go. Your servant will live."

Now where we headed? This guy's on horse back, it won't be just around the corner.

"Lord, don't trouble yourself. I do not deserve that you should have to come under my roof. Just say the word and my servant will be healed."

I wished you could've seen the look on Jesus' face. I didn't know you could surprise him.

"For I am a man," the centurion continued, "under authority, with soldiers under me. I say go and he goes. I say come and he comes."

"I tell you the truth," Jesus put a hand on the man's shoulder and said to the crowd, "I have not found anyone in all of Israel with such great faith.

"Go," Jesus walked the soldier to his horse, "and it will be done just as you have believed."

If only he could say that about me.

The things he taught, and he called me by name to be his apostle, it seemed like he knew everything before it happened. He was calm, but certain about what he did and said. Never a stammer. You would have thought he planned it—nothing caught him off guard—except the centurion. It really looked like Jesus wasn't ready for that. Or, it could be, he was just so impressed with the man that he didn't try to hide his feelings. It doesn't matter, but gave me confidence to know Jesus can have a common response.

"Master," I put my arm on his shoulder, "what do you want from me?"

"That's my favorite question, Simon." Jesus hung his arm on mine. "Do you trust me?"

"Yes, Lord, I trust you."

"That's all I ask. For now."

"Am I to leave everything?"

"Sometimes a man meets his destiny on the road he took to avoid it."

"I see." I didn't, but I knew I should've.

Joanna did have dinner ready. I encouraged, not ordered, most to go home and give Jesus some time. It was a powerful moment for me and Joanna was impressed.

"Simon," Jesus held his dish of roasted lamb and mint sauce, "you are a lucky man. Joanna, thank you, this is dee-lic-ious."

Joanna flushed at the compliment, and I was thrilled Jesus spoke to her. She doesn't need much, but his kind words came at a good time. I knew she'd give me more leeway if she trusted him.

After dinner he went to the roof. After Jo went to bed, I went to the roof steps and bedded down. It was the right the thing to do. I fell asleep hearing his prayers. I didn't understand the language, but they were prayers, I was sure of that.

FIFTEEN

"Where're we going, Master?" I swallowed the last bite of breakfast.

"Nain."

"Nain? That's some walk. What's there? It will take most of the day." Nain was the arm pit of Galilee in my book. I didn't mention that to Jesus. If he's so smart he must know that.

"They need hope. They deserve some hope." Could I argue with that?

As expected, my house was surrounded with men and boys and families. They'd gathered in yards, sat along the street, waiting to see Jesus. The apostles were there. Could I get use to that—apostles? Matthew and his brother James were at the door, they wouldn't want to miss anything. Phillip and Nathaniel were across the street discussing some fine point of Torah, no doubt. Simon the Zealot leaned on his staff with his ever-present suspicious glare. Thaddaeus couldn't calm him down, not that he was different. Judas, dressed as if ready for an audience with Herod, paced with his hands clasped behind his back. James and John sat back to back half asleep under a fig tree. I didn't see Thomas then heard Andrew and him laugh from the roof without a care.

"Let's go, Simon. Ready?" Jesus came from the house and headed to the shore.

Speaking of hope, I'd hoped most of these folks had something better to do than follow us.

"Who wants to go for a walk?" Jesus shouted.

So much for that idea. You'd a thought someone hollered who wants honeycomb to a bunch of school kids. The crowd scrambled to their feet, gathered their children and walking sticks. I was tempted to tell them where we're headed. Which might-a changed their minds.

"Simon," Jesus said, "you have a problem with everyone coming?"

"Me? Nah. Not a bit."

"Glad to hear that. It takes a special man to be a leader, and you can't lead if you don't have followers."

I need to watch what I think, much less what I say.

Children were skipping and kicking rocks. The townspeople that didn't join us waved and brought us bites of dried meat and fish to nibble. We walked through fig trees, olive groves and vineyards, picking fruit. I suspected it looked like locust had feasted in our path. Just north of Tiberius Jesus stopped to pet a stray lamb and told us to rest.

"Where's your mommy little one?" Jesus caressed the lamb like it was his favorite.

"Master, don't we have a long way to go?" I thought I should tell him.

"Which of you," Jesus stroked the bleating lamb, "having lost a sheep would not stop what you are doing and rescue it?" Jesus handed me the sheep. "Simon, see if you can find its mother." Talk about feeling stupid.

Down the hill, I heard its mother's bell and the lamb scurried to the herd with a sheep dog at its heels. I turned back and Jesus headed up the hill and the crowd followed.

"Jesus," I was out of breath, "how are we going to Nain? We can't climb Mt. Tabor. Can we?"

"I thought we would head over to Nazareth for lunch with Mother then south to the city. That meet with your approval?"

Lunch sounded like a good idea. Wait, all these people.

"Uh, what, how is everyone going to eat?"

"Those that have will have to share. Remember what I said about worry?"

"Yes, but—"

"Where's your faith, Simon?"

"What happen to Peter?"

"I wondered the same thing."

Why did I think I'd get a straight answer?

SIXTEEN

I ate too much at Nazareth. Mary, Jesus' mother, you probably remember her, came and dragged Jesus off with Andrew and me. James and John slipped in behind. It looked like she had been cooking all morning.

"Simon, have some of Mom's lentil soup. It's legendary. You will see."

It was more like a stew, so thick and spicy.

"This is dee-li-cious, Mary." I told her.

"Good one Pete." Jesus said.

I was ready for a nap, but that was not on Jesus' schedule.

One good thing, it was downhill to Nain. The town was nothing. You could see most of it in a valley surrounded by foothills. And you could hear the mourners cry as a funeral procession came from the city gate. The sea of black shrouds flapped in the breeze behind a small coffin carried by a man in front and one behind.

"Must be a child." I said to Jesus.

"So sad." He went to a lady, the mother no doubt, behind the casket. She sobbed through her hand clasped to her mouth. Her body shook. I heard sniffles and weeping behind me. Andrew swept pass me, but I stayed put. I was close enough, but couldn't stand still. My feet ignored me as I shuffled closer.

"Don't cry." Jesus said to the mother. But she couldn't stop and collapsed in his arms. "Don't cry," he said again, "it will be all right."

Was he? Could he? Would he? He stepped over and put both hands on the casket and lifted his head. I couldn't hear his prayer. But we all heard this.

"Young man I say to you, get up."

Nothing. I don't know what I expected, but nothing wasn't it. This could be embarrassing and make the mother furious. What if nothing happened? But the lid, the one on the coffin rattled. It shook. I froze. A few gasp later it happened again. I held my breath, but the noisy crowd and sobbing mourners were swarming. The men sat the wooden box on the ground and backed away. Wouldn't you?

The lid flipped off.

"Look, everyone." A boy, the one inside, sat up with his hands straight up. "I'm—not—dead—anymore."

It got real quiet for a minute before his mother let out a screech. Jesus laughed and clapped. The crowd praised

God—shouted Glory, Hallelujah—as the boy jumped and skipped and yelled, "I'm not dead anymore."

I was weak. I'd seen everything. Yes, it was amazing. But, I have to tell you, this was frightening. I stood in the presence of a man that raised the dead in front of my eyes. I stood in the presence of a man that could do anything. If I ever doubted Jesus was the Messiah, I didn't then and I knew I never would.

Do you think—Jesus restored a life—can he take one too?

SEVENTEEN

To be honest, the crowds, and me too, began to expect that Jesus would do amazing things, that was disappointing. I blamed him. Often he told us not to tell anyone. He did things so calmly that you had to think, if he doesn't get all excited, why should I? But it changed one day. I'll get to it, first this you should know.

Ever since Jesus raised that boy from the dead it was impossible for us to go anywhere without people who brought the sick, the cripple, the deaf. Men and women and children with all kinds of diseases.

The possessed were the scariest. They'd bust through the crowd or jump from the hills. They kicked and screamed, foamed at the mouth and shouted curses on the whole lot of us. Jesus was the only one that stood his ground regardless of the threats. He had no compassion when he faced demons.

"Come out," he'd shout, "you are not welcome here anymore."

Every time the demon's screams pierced your senses and threw their victims to the ground in a violent fit.

Remember John the Baptist? We'd not heard a thing about him all year. Then we found out he's Jesus' cousin. Anyway, three of his disciples came and told Jesus that Herod had John thrown in prison because he called Herod an adulterer. I can't go into all that right here but it sounded like John had asked for trouble.

"Master," one said, "John sent us to ask, are you the one, the Messiah, or should he expect someone else?" His own cousin had doubts? I suppose I would too if Jesus left me to rot in jail. He can raise the dead. Why doesn't he rescue his cousin from prison?

"Go back and report to John what you hear and see." Jesus looked torn, as if he wanted to go with them. "The blind received their sight, the lame walk, lepers are cured, deaf hear, dead are raised and good news is preached to the poor."

John's disciples praised God and left.

"Simon, or is it Peter?" Nathaniel, with his so important attitude said through his teeth. "Do you know where that came from?"

"What? Where what came from?"

"Jesus just quoted the prophet Isaiah. Surely you remember from your years of schooling."

I shouldn't do this but you should know, Nathaniel wants everyone to know he's a scholar. But I want you to know something else—

"Nathaniel, how old are you?"

"I'll be forty soon. Why?"

"Just wondered how long it took you to become a complete jackass." That shut him up, temporarily.

"Simon, when you're through." Jesus caught me.

"What did you go out in the wilderness to see?" He said to all. "A reed swayed by the wind? A man dressed in fine cloths? Then what? A prophet? Yes, I tell you and more than a prophet. This is the one of whom Malachi wrote. 'I will send my messenger ahead of you, who will prepare the way before you.' I tell you there is none born of woman that is greater than John."

"Nathaniel, then why is John in jail?"

"I, I don't know, Simon?"

Hah, something he doesn't know.

EIGHTEEN

Seldom did Jesus answer a question unless it was with a question, or story. When a Pharisee, named Simon, no relation, asked Jesus to dinner we went. That was one of the best things about traveling with Jesus, we ate well.

Jesus reclined at the table and we found a place and sat. Then a woman, I'm not pointing fingers, but the way she dressed, I suspected she worked at night if you get my drift, came and sat behind Jesus. She was weeping. She wiped Jesus' feet with her hair, she really did. She kissed his feet and opened a bottle of perfume, there was no doubt, the smell filled the room, a relief with this bunch. Everyone watched as she poured perfume on Jesus' feet.

"If your teacher is really a prophet." The Pharisee leaned too close for my liking. "He would know who that woman is that's touched him, that she's a sinner"

"Why is she in your house in the first place?" I thought that was a good question.

"Simon, I have something to tell you."

"Yes, Lord." I sat up.

"Not you. I'm speaking to our host."

"Go on." The Pharisee said. He sounded like he'd been caught with his hand in the honey jar.

"There were two men who owed money to a moneylender. One owed five hundred denarii and the other owed fifty. Neither of them could pay their loans, so the moneylender cancelled their debt."

I need to borrow from that man.

"Which of them," Jesus went on, "will love him more?"

You know, sometimes Jesus asked dumb questions. No disrespect, but I wanted to blurt out the answer. The Pharisee beat me to it.

"Why, the one who had the bigger debt. Of course."

I knew that.

"Of course. You answered right." Then Jesus turned to the woman.

What now?

"I came into your house," Jesus said, "and you did not give me water for my feet. But she, the moment I came in, wet my feet with her tears and wiped them with her hair. You did not greet me with a kiss, but she has not stopped kissing my feet. You did not put oil on my head, but she poured perfume on my feet. Hear me, her many sins are forgiven—for she loved me much. But he who has been forgiven little—loves little."

Our host should've been embarrassed, but he looked indignant.

"You sins are forgiven." Jesus said to the woman to my bewilderment.

It wasn't just me, murmurs surrounded the table. Who is this who forgives sin?

"Your faith has saved you, go in peace." He told her and that was that.

Where does that leave me?

NINETEEN

There's no way I could tell you everything. There wouldn't be books enough to hold it. It would take me a lifetime. And I'd need a scribe. My writing is, well not educated.

Who could get use to the fact that just when you think you have him figured out, he does something new? I told you he told stories. Some of them are still a mystery even when I'd heard them before.

He had a lot of them on the Kingdom of Heaven. There was one about a mustard seed. One about yeast and a woman. One about weeds and good seed. There was another one about grain. But the one he told about the Samaritan you have to hear me tell it.

There was a lawyer, a teacher of the law listening to Jesus. It was late and Jesus looked like he wanted to be done when the lawyer spoke.

"Teacher," the lawyer fluffed his scraggly beard, puffing through his fat lips, "what must I do to gain eternal life?" Not a bad question, I admit.

"The law." Jesus had a question for him—no surprise. "What is written in the law? How is it that you see it?"

"The law, my specialty." He shot out his chin, stroked his beard and squinted his eyes. "It says precisely, 'You must love the Lord your God with all your heart, with all your soul, with all your strength and with all your mind.' As recorded in the fifth book, Deuteronomy." He looked at Jesus for the first time and added in a hurry, "And, your neighbor as your self."

Aha, did you hear? He had the answer all along. An expert in the law. This was no legitimate question in the first place. Isn't that just like a lawyer? He asked a question when he already knew the answer.

"Good," Jesus said, "go, and do likewise and you will live."

That's it? Did Jesus say that all we need do to get to heaven is this? You might ask, why did he tell all those stories about the kingdom if all we need to know and do is love God with all … ah, not so fast.

"But," the lawyer was back at it, "that brings up another question. Who—might be—my neighbor?" He said with dripping disdain.

Who is my neighbor? This jerk was yanking my anchor. But Jesus looked glad to hear this.

"There was a certain man," Jesus said, "headed from Jerusalem down to Jericho, who fell among thieves."

This was not news. With Herod's temple completed last year, the workers and slaves who came from all over Judea were out of work and half of them lived in the wilderness along the Jericho road robbing travelers without mercy.

"The thieves grabbed the man," Jesus grabbed a stunned young man. "They beat him." Jesus shook the man. The crowd liked that. "They ripped off his clothes." Jesus pulled the man's cloak. "They stole his money." Jesus grabbed the man's purse and held it high. "And they left him for dead." A few gasped as Jesus pushed the man down. No, he didn't hurt the fellow.

"By chance," Jesus held the man, "a certain priest came that way but passed by keeping his distance." Hmmm, another jerk. Jesus looked like he enjoyed this, but the lawyer looked bored. But lawyers normally look bored.

"There came another man that way, a Levite," Jesus said, "but he passed by on the other side."

I'm surrounded with jerks.

"But," Jesus eyed the lawyer, "a certain Samaritan came that way."

You should've seen the lawyers face twisted in disgust when Jesus said "Samaritan." Prejudice is nothing new, especially in religious matters. Pharisees despised Samaritans. Neither would cross paths if they could help it. But the lawyer no longer looked bored—bowels blocked perhaps—but not bored. I had no idea where Jesus was headed, but everyone was glued to the story. Everyone except, guess who.

"The Samaritan was moved with compassion and stopped." Jesus said with his back to the lawyer as if he couldn't stand the sight of him. "He bound up the man's wounds."

Sorry, but I have to interrupt, there was something about the way Jesus told this story. It didn't feel like a story, One, because it could've happened. Two, because Jesus was spellbinding, and three, he acted this out right in front of us. Back to the story.

"He poured oil and wine on the wounds." Jesus pulled his helper to his feet. "He put the man on his donkey and took him to town."

Can't you just see this?

"The Samaritan brought him to an inn." And each time Jesus said "Samaritan" the lawyer shuddered. "He cared for the man all night." This man sounds more like Jesus than a Samaritan.

"The next day," Jesus took two coins from the man's purse and handed them to another, "the man gave the innkeeper two denarii and told him, 'take care of the man while I'm gone. Whatever he needs, and I'll pay the cost when I return.'"

Two denarii? That's a day's wage. That would pay for a room for a month. This Samaritan must be loaded.

"Which of these," Jesus faced the lawyer, "was a neighbor to the man who fell among the thieves?"

This simple question drew approval from the crowd. The lawyer looked annoyed or angry or both.

"I suppose," the lawyer said with a huff, "that fellow who showed mercy."

I suppose? This jerk is giving a whole new meaning to the word jerk.

Jesus waited, but the lawyer was done—I don't think he got it. Even I understood. Anyone is our neighbor, but I guessed the lawyer was a neighbor to no one. One more thing, the lawyer couldn't bring himself to say the word, Samaritan. No hope for him,

I have another one about Jericho, with a better ending. Especially for a certain tax collector. Yes, another tax collector—and this isn't a story—I was there.

"What is it with Jesus and tax collectors, Andy? If it's not tax collectors it's harlots. This is not who I expected to be with."

"Some would say the same about you." Andrew was proud of that one.

TWENTY

We took that same road from Jerusalem to Jericho, of course, there was only one road to start with. There were seven or eight hundred with us which choked the road and filled the air with dust. And the noise of jibber-jabber was like a lake full of women with their week of wash.

The main gate to Jericho was jammed with people. Word had gotten out we were coming. Just for the record this is the same Jericho that Joshua commanded the walls to fall with shouting and trumpets' blasts—in case you don't know that.

As we approached the crowd calmed but you could hear one man in a panic.

"Jesus, Son of David, have mercy on me."

We couldn't see him behind the crowd. They tried to quiet the man, but he would not be quiet.

"Jesus, Son of David, have mercy on me."

"Simon," Jesus pushed me toward the voice, "find him and bring him here,"

I don't think I'll get use to taking orders, but I went. The man was blind. His eye lids fluttered over his milky eyes. He held out his hands looking for a way through the crowd.

"Come with me, the Teacher is calling for you." You'd a thought God himself called the man. He froze.

"Bartimaeus go." Two men stepped aside. Bartimaeus dropped his coat and latched on to my arm with a death grip. We made our way to Jesus. He released me and groped the air looking for Jesus.

"What do you ask of me?"

"Master, healer, you have the power to cure me of my blindness."

"You're faith," Jesus took the man's face in his hands, "has healed you. Go in peace."

Bartimaeus shielded his eyes. He turned his hands as if seeing them for the first time.

"Praise the God of Miracles." His eyes opened as wide as his smile. "Praise Jehovah. I can see, I can see."

"Bartimaeus can see. He can see." Came the uproar for him—for the miracle.

Jesus moved to town and the whole city came. Bartimaeus looked at everything for the first time.

"Who touched me?" Jesus stopped.

This happened before. And like before I thought this an amusing question. There were so many pressing in it could have been anyone and I told him.

"Yes, I know, Simon but it wasn't anyone. It's a woman at death's door. I felt the strength go out from me."

He looked for her. She stood still as a stick.

"Did you touch me?" Jesus asked her.

"I did, yes sir it was me. I'm sorry." She trembled.

"Don't be afraid, I want to thank you. Your faith has healed you."

She fell to her knees but Jesus lifted her and smothered her in his arms, his face to hers, and he whirled her around. She cried and laughed and sang and raised her hands and twirled and praised God. The crowd whooped and hollered and praised God and swung each other around without a care.

Bartimaeus was right in the middle of it as Jesus continued and the throng followed, no doubt expecting another miracle. It was all in a day's work for Jesus. I know that's rude, but it was no longer a surprise. Jesus didn't plan these things, people came and Jesus did what needed to be done. He didn't try to keep it quiet anymore, not that he could, that's why crowds surrounded him. He didn't get a minute's peace. I don't know how he kept it up. At times he was exhausted and frustrated, perhaps angry, but I never saw him refuse to touch or heal or encourage.

Jesus could laugh for all he was worth. More rare these days, but laugh he did in Jericho. No, not at Bartimaeus or that woman, and not at the crowd. It was a scrawny little man that gave Jesus one of his best days.

We came to the center square shaded by a sycamore tree. People sat, stood, crowded in. Me and the men, it took the twelve of us, grabbed hands and pushed back the crowd and made space for Jesus. We knew he wanted to speak. But, when he came into the circle he turned and looked into the tree. He chuckled at first, then laughed as if he'd seen the funniest thing in his life. Confused, I looked at Andrew and John and Thomas. They shrugged.

I saw him. A man straddled a limb that overhung the crowd. I wondered why he'd be up a tree unless to hide. He picked the wrong tree today. He was dressed in a gaudy robe, fancy hat and jewelry dangled from his neck.

"It's Zacchaeus." Someone said.

"Taxman." Another said. Or should I say hissed.

"Zacchaeus," Jesus called, "come on down. I'm hungry and will eat at your house today."

Another tax collector? We will go to his house? Zacchaeus slid down and landed in a clump in front of Jesus. When he stood, I saw why he was up a tree. He barely came to Jesus' chest.

"Come to my house?" He jumped up, broke through the crowd. "Yes, all of you. We will have a feast."

"Is this Jesus going to eat at a sinner's house?" A man poked me.

"Looks like he is."

Half the crowd straggled off as Jesus headed to the market with Zacchaeus. Zacchaeus dashed up and down, ordered this and that and paid the merchants from his fat purse.

"Jesus, you can come anytime, all of you, all the food and drink will be delivered straight away." The crowd apparently changed their minds when Zacchaeus announced free food.

Zacchaeus' house was up a hill beside a stream. Big house, with servants outside tending to his garden and goats. A horse drawn cart rumbled by from the market and was met by more servants standing ready.

Inside was filled with just the kind you might expect in a tax collector's house. More tax collectors from the looks of it, and it didn't take a genius to see there were harlots looking right at home.

Bartimaeus came. Then the woman Jesus healed. Followed by the religious who swooped in with haughty hats and robes. Reminded me of Matthew's house. But I knew nobody could be ready for what happened. Maybe not Jesus either.

"Master." Zacchaeus stepped to the middle of the room and stood on a stool.

"Everyone quiet. Zacchaeus has something to say."

"Thank you. Master, I want to give half of everything I own to the poor." Stunned doesn't explain the feeling in the air. Someone choke on food. A goblet bounced. Two tax collectors collapsed.

"Are you sure, Zacchaeus?" Was Jesus shocked?

"And, anyone that I've cheated, I'll repay them twice, no three, no, four times the amount." Zacchaeus was beaming. Jesus stared. I wished Zacchaeus had cheated me. Other tax collectors grunted and held their heads in pain.

"Today," Jesus stood by Zacchaeus, "salvation has come to this house, because this man too is a son of Abraham. For," now Jesus was beaming, "the Son of Man came to seek and to save that which was lost."

Zacchaeus shouted to his servants and they dashed about serving the food and wine. Music filled the air and people danced. I assumed Zacchaeus would be one of us after this but more importantly Jesus' words churned in my head. "I came to seek and to save, son of Abraham, salvation has come to this house."

TWENTY ONE

I beg your forgiveness—well not beg—I ask your forgiveness, which isn't easy for me. I have completely jumped over two, no three of the most important events you could imagine.

One day, we were up to several thousand, and this day was the largest. Enough to start a city. People followed for days. Many came from out of the area but many were from nearby towns a day at a time. It's difficult to describe. A whole hillside littered with families and shepherds and shop-owners and merchants. There were men from the groves. There were slaves and beggars. There were many that I had seen healed—they followed of course. And the ever present gaggle of priests. Also I saw some that didn't want be seen. I wondered if they were criminals or other scoundrels afraid of being thrown in jail. Maybe Zealots? Children ran about without a care. Babies complained at the noon day sun.

Jesus taught much of the day and healed any that were brought. There was no end to what he would do for these people. It was late, I'm talking sun-setting. The people were restless. Mothers rummaged for something to feed their little ones.

"Master." Someone needed to tell him. "The hour is late. Don't you see these people need to eat? Send them into town so they can buy some food."

"Simon, why don't you give them something to eat?"

"Me? What can I do? How much will it cost?"

That was only a few comments I could think for his absurd suggestion when a boy tugged my cloak.

"You can have them." He poked a basket in my gut.

"What do you have there, Simon?" Jesus reached out.

"A basket. The boy's basket. His lunch it looks like. There is, let me see, five barley loaves and two salted fish, that's it. What good is that?"

"Men, have the people sit."

Now it got strange. Jesus took the basket as the crowd sat covering the hillside. He lifted the lad's lunch and said, "Thank you, Father for your faithfulness."

That's it?

He took a loaf of bread and broke it into two pieces.

"Judas, you and Phillip find a basket and take these and give it to the people, and ask them to share."

I heard what he said. Was he serious? There were five loaves, little loaves at that, the size of my fist. This could infuriate the people. Only one or two would get a taste and the others would wonder why Jesus would feed a few. And he said to tell them to share. Share what? If they took one bite what would be left to share? I was embarrassed for him.

He reached in the basket and took another loaf. He broke this one and held the pieces as Andrew and John took the bits in their baskets and Jesus told them the same thing, "Give it to the people. Ask them to share."

"Simon, here." Matthew flopped a basket in my lap. "You going to help?"

"And make a fool of myself. No thanks. Don't you see he'll be out of bread when the next three loaves are gone?"

Matthew grabbed a loaf along with Thomas and stepped into the crowd. I looked for Andrew and John but had to stand. They were down the hill still passing out bread. I scratched my beard and looked in the boy's basket in Jesus' hand. It was full. The rest of the men came and took a loaf for their baskets and off they went. But they didn't have just one loaf. I was in a fog.

"Simon, what are you waiting for?" Jesus tossed a loaf in my basket. "And take this too." He stuck in a fish and gave me a shove.

I saw those near me had several chucks of bread so I reached for the fish and heard Jesus chuckle. What was so funny? My basket got heavy. It was full—overflowing— loaves of bread and a dozen fish. Instantly I remembered the day on the sea when Jesus filled my net after we'd fished all night and caught nothing. Now my basket is full. Maybe someday I'll do what I'm told—maybe.

I passed the fish and the bread and the folks took some and passed some. My basket did run out, but not until everyone, and I mean everyone had all they could eat. Yes, I stole a bite or two, or three, as I passed the food.

Jesus told us to pick up what was left—get this—we collected twelve baskets full. One basket for each of us. Food we didn't need. I didn't know any better so I gave mine to the boy who started this in the first place.

I thought this would be the end of the day, but the crowd pushed forward. They weren't mad or a mob, but they reached for Jesus.

"Men, we need to leave." Jesus got no argument from us.

"What is wrong with them, you just fed the lot of them." James said.

"They think they want me to be their king."

"Does that surprise you?" I said.

"Not like this. Not now. Men, go. Get in the boat and go ahead of me. I'll join you later. I need to pray."

It was impossible to tell his mood. He couldn't be afraid of the crowd, not Jesus. He wasn't angry, but seemed frustrated. I'd never seen him so exhausted. Matthew started to say something, but Jesus pointed to the water.

TWENTY-TWO

I had no idea how he would join us later, but his go meant go. We piled in the boat. The men collapsed on the deck or flopped against the sides. I slid between Thaddeus and the Zealot. Andrew hoisted the sail and I steered us into the murky water and moonlit night. We were too many for my boat, even small waves splashed over the gunnels. But it was a short trip and I knew it well. Just like I know the Galilee—I thought.

A blast of wind slipped up on me. I didn't see the telltale ripples, so couldn't steer into the wind. The gust rocked us. Everyone scrambled to grab a rail, a seat, a something.

"Andrew, get that sail down and tied off. They'll be another." I told him.

And there was. Only this time it wasn't a gust. It just blew, pitching my boat like a leaf. I sat in the stern and wrapped both arms around the tiller. My only hope to keep us upright was to anticipate the swells. The Galilee is famous for gales but I never expected this since it was

Jesus that told us to get in the boat. Shouldn't he know we would be in danger?

"Men, move to the front, we're taking on water." I shouted over the howling wind. Not concerned for myself, but I had a boatload. "Keep an eye out for any light on shore, I need to know when we cleared the point at Magdala."

"Simon, I hate to tell you, but the wind's from the west. We're blowing to the middle of the lake." Thomas was right.

"It'll pass." James tried to keep us calm.

"Hang on." John said the obvious as I remembered another storm—the one that took my father. It was as fierce as this and I realized we could all end up at the bottom with him. Fish-food for all Jesus would know. What was he thinking?

"Andrew put up a bit of sail, I have no control over this thing. No, better yet, James, drop the anchor off the bow to flip us around and take the waves. I was not ready to die. The waves crashed over the bow. Freezing rain smacked the deck. Lightning cracked the sky. We were tossed around the angry sea, frightened for our lives, drenched to the bone.

"Simon, light, I see light." Matthew was shivering from the cold or fright or both.

But it was more than a light.

"Fellows, is that a man—is that a ghost?"

Now what? I was terrified. Was Father back from the deep? Should I jump and end it?

"Don't be afraid, it is I." Is it—him? I didn't know whether to be thrilled or furious.

"Well, Lord, if it's you, tell me to come to you on the water." That should settle it.

"Come."

He said it. I'd asked for it, and just angry enough to do it. I swung my leg over the side. My fingers clenching the boat. White knuckles against the worn wood. I'd lost my mind. The others stared in agreement. Fear gripped me, but when my foot touched the water it was, how can I explain, it was firm. Yet I felt the frigid water slapping my foot.

"Simon, don't be ridiculous." But Judas was too late. This was a point of pride.

I swung my other leg over expecting to plunge to my neck, but stood. The best I can explain, it felt like sloshing sand. Over my shoulder Jesus waited. One hand off. One half step to Jesus. My other hand held tight—unwilling to let go. My heart was on fire but I let loose and took one more step. I felt like a hatchling thrown from its nest to certain death. But with each step, I stood taller. Then a gust pounded me. I took my eyes off Jesus. I saw the waves and got that sinking feeling. I would drown.

"Lord save me." My only hope.

"Simon," he grabbed me, "why did you doubt?"

With one touch he raised me from certain death to stand on the waves. The storm stopped. We were in the boat. Next we were on shore—just like that.

But his question echoed, "why did you doubt?" Good question, he wasn't the one sinking. Jesus had more faith in me than I did in him.

Before you get all righteous, hear this, at least I got out of the boat. No, it wasn't enough for the men. They were fawning over Jesus. What about me? He wasn't the one who nearly drowned. It was me. Yeah, yeah, yeah, I was in over my head because of my big mouth—again. I was so sure. But for only four steps. He had to save me.

The men had a big laugh, but Jesus didn't. He was disappointed. I have to give him that. But whether I deserve it or not, I was humiliated. If only I'd stayed where I belonged. Who do I think I am walking on water? And who does he think he is letting me sink? Just like my father this was a set up—to what—prove I was low on the faith scale? I have a good mind to do it. That'll show them. I bet they're jealous and hoped I would drown.

I need this? Another failure. And why would I think Jesus would give me a second chance? I'll remind him that he called me. He chose me. None of this was my idea.

You know what? Enough. It's not like I can't go back to fishing. He's got plenty to choose from. Thousand follow him. He has his pick. Why would I want to hang around this bunch? A tax collector, a rug merchant, a zealot, and harlots. They aren't my kind. I have a life, a business, a wife. She believes in me and will be thrilled to have me back home like a normal person.

First thing in the morning, I'll say my goodbyes. Thanks, but no thanks. I have better things to do. It's been nice, but …

TWENTY THREE

"Simon, come with us." Jesus said with a hint of sadness. "We're going to take a few days off. I need to think some things through."

I should have told him I'm through.

"Simon Peter, I want you to go."

"Maybe tomorrow, you go ahead." I'm such a coward.

"All right, we will wait."

Now what? Trapped again.

I'll talk this over with Joanna. Two minutes ago I was so sure I'd quit this—this, whatever I was doing—and go on with my life. What would make me a follower of a holyman. Nothing. I've always been my own man. Not that I'd tell Jesus, but I admit I'm a sinner. Shouldn't that disqualify me? No, I haven't done anything that bad. A little lusting, yes. I may have hedged a little on my taxes. I might have overcharged a customer—not much. I've picked a fight or two—or more. I'm prone to cursing, but that's Father's fault. I should blame him for everything, but that won't work with Jesus. I haven't killed anyone. I haven't stolen. I haven't' committed adultery. I'm not so bad. But I'll never measure up. I'll sleep on this. Make my decision in the morning—again. Things will make sense then.

"Simon, you're going to stay the night? Where is everyone?"

"Yes, I told Jesus, I'll see him in the morning. Joanna—you get better looking everyday."

"Why don't you relax, wash up, I'll get dinner, go." She gave me playful nudge. What a great lady. I knew I wasn't going to object or tell her anything until I knew something myself, assuming I would.

SCENE THREE

Footsteps of St. Peter

The Gospel Years

Who do you say he is?

TWENTY FOUR

"I'm here. Where to?" I sat by Jesus hoping the others didn't know why they waited.

Have you ever found yourself in over your head and have no idea what the right decision is? Yes, I know that in-over-your-head comment is personal. I only showed up because he insisted he'd wait. If I didn't they'd like nothing better than to jabber behind my back all the way to—

"Just where are we going?"

"I thought Caesarea Philippi, it's majestic. A place for us to rest a few days." He threw his blanket over my shoulder and took off with me on his heals. "If that's alright with you, Peter."

"There you go again with that Peter thing. You know it'll take all day?" I would have bit my tongue, but it had one callus too many.

"Simon, is that another sandal in your mouth." Ah yes, Nathaniel with a jab. Big surprise.

Jesus could not have picked a better day, but he was not in the best of moods and didn't try to hide it. I give him credit for dealing with this bunch.

I should tell you more about the men. I've told you Nathaniel was a know-it-all, but did I tell you he was usually right? That made him all the harder to stomach. James and John were a handful, constantly looking to dunk the unsuspecting and laugh till they hurt, but the best partners a man could want. Simon the Zealot was still a mystery and still hid a dagger acting like Jesus' bodyguard, as if he couldn't take care of himself. Young Phillip would believe anything if it wasn't for Thomas. Thomas was no pushover. He wanted every detail. Matthew was a kid again without a care in the world. I envied him that. Judas on the other hand I didn't trust even if Jesus did. Jesus had him keep the purse which I thought was a huge mistake, but he didn't ask me. James, the other James, Son of Alphaeus, Matthew's brother, was the quiet one, almost as if he thought he wasn't good enough to be with Jesus. He may have a secret or two. Thaddaeus was the most changed man of all, even compared to Matthew. He'd been bitter and mean to everyone. Particularly to his two sons, which kept me riled and running to their rescue. But he became a servant to any and to all. He'd tote your bag or coat, you name it, waving off any thank-yous.

Andrew, my little brother Andy, was the best. He'd quit ribbing me altogether and proud to have me around.

That made me proud of him. He seldom offered his opinion. I remember the day he said about the Baptizer, "I just want more of him." I say, Jesus got all of Andrew, his best pick in my book.

A few others straggled with us till we turned east toward Bethsaida then turned back and I was glad. This was more like it. Just the twelve and Jesus. Although I was in good shape, and so were many of us, we had to push to keep up. He was a man on a mission.

Three years? Could that be? How much longer?

I watched his wide strides and still wondered who he was. He has to be the Messiah, he just has to be with all the miracles. But it's so odd to be walking along with a bunch of men and a messiah.

"Teacher," two men, practically dragging another said, "can you cure this man? He's blind."

We were in Bethsaida.

"Is he dumb, too?" I told you Jesus was in a foul mood. "Can he speak for himself?"

"Yes, but he asked us to bring him to you."

"Is that right?" Jesus took the blind man's arm.

"I didn't want to bother you, Lord?" The man was trembling.

People gathered to see what Jesus would do.

"Did you come to see a trick? Do you think you can test me?" Jesus often spoke to Pharisees like this, but not to a crowd. He knew their thoughts. These people have no idea who they are playing with.

"James, John, Simon Peter, Andrew, help me." He led the man outside the town away from the crowd and any chance of a spectacle.

I don't expect you to believe me, but Jesus spit in the man's eyes. It's a good thing the man was blind. If he saw who spit on him I might need to protect Jesus. That's a good way to get slugged.

The man said he could see, but not clearly. So Jesus bent over and got some clay. He spit in the clay—made spittle and placed his hands on the man's eyes and prayed. He took his hands from the man's eyes, and the man said he could see Jesus perfectly.

"My Lord, what can I do for you?" He knelt.

"Go tell your family what has been done. And never fail to give glory to God."

"Andrew, tell the others we will meet them in Caesarea Philippi. Men stay with me. We have a few miles yet."

TWENTY FIVE

I had lived in Bethsaida thirteen years, but never came to this beautiful place. No wonder Jesus brought us here. The lush ferns and palm trees and brilliant sycamores surrounded a waterfall that fed a secluded pool. The sound alone could calm a madman.

"Men," Jesus said as the others arrived. "Who do the others say that I am?" No one rushed to answer and I thought, who cares what people think.

"Some say, you are John the Baptist raised from the dead." It was Nathaniel. Are you surprised? "And some say you are Elijah."

"Still others say," Phillip jumped in, "you are Jeremiah—"

"Or one of the other prophets." Nathaniel would not be outdone. Jerk comes back to mind.

There was a nervous quiet.

"Then let me ask you," Jesus looked at me—through me, "who do you say that I am?"

More quiet as I wondered why he'd asked such a simple question. Or was it? Interesting no one said, what many said, that he is—liar—lunatic—fake. I realized what he was doing. What he may be best at. Making us think for ourselves, because we'd heard it all.

The Pharisees accused him of being possessed. His own brothers rumored he was losing his mind. And how many times had we heard, 'he's Mary's son, a carpenter leading fools astray.' No wonder he said 'who do *you* say I am?'

"You are the Christ. Son of the living God." All of Caesarea Philippi could have heard me. It felt amazing to say that. But the best—Jesus rushed to hug me and I swear, I felt his tears on my face.

"Simon, bless you, son of Jonah. This was not revealed to you by flesh and blood, but by my Father in heaven. Now—you—are—Peter. On this rock I will build my sanctuary. The gates of Hades will not overcome it. You have the keys of the Kingdom. Whatever you bind on earth will be bound in heaven. Whatever you loose on earth will be loosed in heaven.

"But it is not time for the world to know who I am."

"When Lord?" I was filled with something I can't explain. But I knew what I said had given Jesus the greatest joy. And me too.

Simon the Zealot had made a fire as twilight seeped in.

"Come, my friends, I have more to tell you." We sat around the fire like school kids with their teacher.

"In a few days," joy left his face, "we will go to Jerusalem. It is time for me to suffer many things at the hands of the chief priests, the scribes and the Pharisees. I will be killed. But I promise you I will come again."

Have you ever felt your heart burn—about to burst?

"No. Lord, never." It was as if my son had died again.

"Simon Peter, you do not have your mind on the things of God, but on the things of man. Get behind me. Men, if any want to be my disciple, you must deny yourself and take up your cross and follow me. I tell you the truth, some of you will not taste death before you see the Son of Man enter his glory.

"We leave for Jerusalem tomorrow. Rest, you will need it."

Rest?

About the Author

Mac's bio and ministry information can be found at: www.way.org.

His one-man Biblical dramas range from 25 to 90 minutes and includes;

> The Gospel According to Simon Peter
> Last Words of St. Paul
> Forever Changed (Zacchaeus)
> Nicodemus
> Judas Lives (Fall 2011)

Mac also has a business motivation presentation, What Are You Working For, based on his award winning Artful Framer Gallery. The multi store art business faced bankruptcy, but survived on a 3,000 year old principle to win the Miami Herald's Small Business of the Year, and featured in Inc. Magazine. He loves to tell this story.

For personal; appearances, including book signings please email, info@way.org. Your personal remarks are welcome.

Mac's books are available at most Christian bookstores and on your favorite on-line bookstores. Barnes and Noble stores will gladly order his books for you.

Books stores please contact, Ingram, Anchor Distributors and STL-Distribution.

Other Books from One Way Books

Title: The Isle of Eden
Author: Kay Dorenbos
ISBN 9781936459018
Price $14.95

A romantic Christian Fantasy that reads like an arm-chair vacation to the tropics. Will the marooned pilot stay on the island with the woman he loves, or return to the "real" world to save his dying brother?

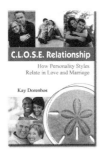

Title: C.L.OS.E. Relationship
Author: Kay Dorenbos
ISBN 9781936459032
Price $12.95

Kay brings 46 years of marriage and 30 years of Temperament Training into her examination of conflict resolution and marital harmony. She has developed "user friendly" terms to describe the five per-

PALESTINE

Roman Miles
0 5 10 20 30 40

English Miles
0 5 10 20 30 40

S Y R I

Danaba
Helbon
DAMASCUS
Chrysorrhoas (Abana)
R. Pharpar
R. Abana
Chalcis
CŒLE-SYRIA
Abila
Hermon
Phæno
Trachonitis
Saphet
Mons Alsadamus
Neapolis
Canatha
Dionysias
Philippi
Bostra
Adraah
Zorra (Bozra)
Auranitis
Nebo
Gaulanitis
Cæsarea Philippa (Paneas)
Dan
Sogane
R. Jordan
L. Phiala
Seleucia
Samochonitis
Ashtaroth
Bergasa
Gamala
Hieromax
Abila
Arbela
Gadara
Bethsaida (Julias)
S. of Galilee L. of Gennesareth or Tiberias
Tarichea Amathus
Aulon
Jordan
Kedesh
Chorazin
Capernaum
Bethsaida
Tiberias
Amathus
Gischala
Arbela
Meiron
Mt. Tabor
Gabara
Itabyrion
Jotapata
Gadara
Caia
Sepphoris
Nazareth
Dabaritta
Endor
Nain
Esdraelon
Scythopolis
GALILEE
Heldua
R. Tamyras
Porphyreon
R. Bostrenus
Sidon
Ornithonpolis
Sarepta
Tyre
Alexandroschene
Ecdippa
Ptolemais
Sycaminos
Mt. Carmel
M. Kishon
Dor
Maximianopolis
CÆSAREA
PHŒNICE
GALILEE

(MEDITERRANEAN) SEA

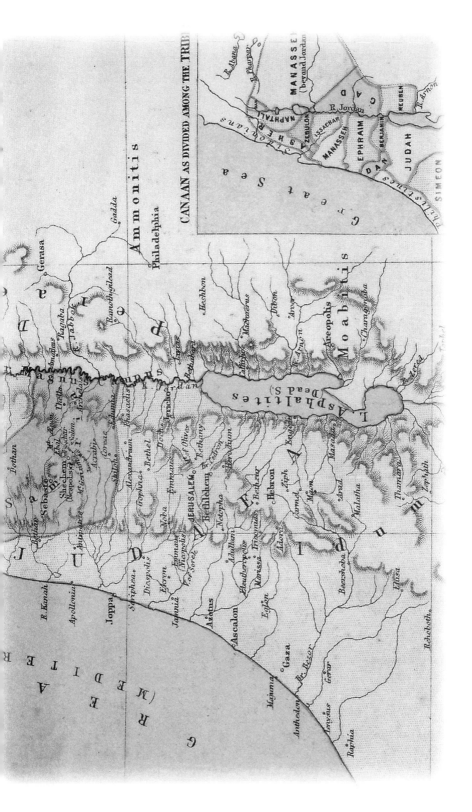

CANAAN AS DIVIDED AMONG THE TRIB[ES]

Great Sea

R. Abana
R. Pharpar
R. Jordan
R. Arnon

MANASSEH (beyond Jordan)
NAPHTALI
ZEBULON
ISSACHAR
MANASSEH
EPHRAIM
DAN
BENJAMIN
JUDAH
SIMEON
ASHER
GAD
REUBEN
PHILISTINES

Ammonitis
Gerasa
Gadla
Philadelphia

Moabitis
Heshbon
Medebar
Dibon
Aroer
Arnon
Areopolis
Charagmoba
Betharu

Peræa
Ragaba
R. Jabbok
Ramothgilead
Pella
Bethsuri

Decapolis
Gadara
Scythopolis
Abila
R. Jordan

Asphaltites
(Dead S.)

Masada

Dothan
Sebaste
Samaria
Shechem
Mt. Ebal
Mt. Gerizim
Sychar
Neapolis
Acrabu
Cornæ
Shiloh
Alexandrium
Archelais
Russcelis

Bethel
Dok
Jericho
Ophrah
Bethabara
Noba
Gophna
Emmaus
Nicopolis
Bethany
Mt. Olivet
JERUSALEM
Bethlehem
Bethphage
Bethphage
Bethzur
Hebron
Tekoa
Bethsur
Carmel
Ziph
Maon
Arad
Malatha
Engaddi
Thamara
Zoar
Zaphith

Samaria
Judæa

Bethabara

Scythopolis
Diospolis
Ekron
Emmaus
Nicopolis
Ramleh
Jamnia
Vor Sorec
Anathoth
Zanoah
Marisa
Eleutheropolis
Betogabra
Timnath
Adora
Bethlet

Ascalon
Ashdod
Eglon
Adora
Gerar
R. Besor
Beersheba
Khusa
Rehoboth

Idumæa

Joppa
Apollonia
R. Kanah
Striphæa

MEDITERRANEAN (G)

Majuma
Gaza
Anthedon
Jenysus
Raphia